PRAISE FOR

"Suspenseful and sublime, *Fog* is a powerful novel of intrigue and love, family and friendship in which fog is a feeling 'like a tenderness of the soul.' Grounded in place with exquisite detail and held aloft by an inspiring worldview, this is a story with unforgettable characters whose entanglements lead us through the magically rendered streets of Montréal and across continents in search of adventure and truth."—Cora Siré, author of *Behold Things Beautiful* and other books.

"Sometimes the fog is a moist mist which beautifully frames our deepest intimacies, sometimes it is a translucent curtain drawn to mask the pain of exile and displacement, and sometimes it is an obscuring darkness where all moral movement seems impossible. But Rana Bose's characters join together to find new ways forward. They emerge from the fog by recognizing the history of 'the Main' while seeing it anew." —Michael Springate, author of *The Beautiful West & The Beloved of God*.

"... suspenseful, conflicting, mysterious and hard to put down. (…) A literate mystery/thriller set in Montreal (on 'the Main') with side trips to Calcutta and Kandahar, this is a superbly written book about a neighbourhood, friendships, justice and belonging. Highly recommended."—James Fisher, *The Miramichi Rader*

Fog

OTHER BOOKS BY RANA BOSE

Recovering Rude
The Fourth Canvas
The Death of Abbie Hoffman and other Plays
Five or Six Characters in Search of Toronto

RANA BOSE

Fog

A Novel

Baraka
Books

Montréal

ISBN 978-1-77186-184-7 pbk; 978-1-77186-189-2 epub; 978-1-77186-190-8 pdf; 978-1-77186-191-5 mobi pocket

Cover and back cover photos by Jacques Nadeau
Book Design by Folio infographie
Editing and proofreading: Robin Philpot, Arielle Aaronson, Nick Fonda

Legal Deposit, 2nd quarter 2019

Bibliothèque et Archives nationales du Québec
Library and Archives Canada

Published by Baraka Books of Montreal
6977, rue Lacroix
Montréal, Québec H4E 2V4
Telephone: 514 808-8504
info@barakabooks.com

Printed and bound in Quebec

Trade Distribution & Returns
Canada and the United States
Independent Publishers Group
1-800-888-4741 (IPG1);
orders@ipgbook.com

We acknowledge the support from the Société de développement des entreprises culturelles (SODEC) and the Government of Quebec tax credit for book publishing administered by SODEC.

Société
de développement
des entreprises
culturelles
Québec

Financé par le gouvernement du Canada
Funded by the Government of Canada | Canadä

"In the most absolute tranquillity or in the midst of tumultuous events, in safety or danger, in innocence or corruption, we are a crowd of others."

–Elena Ferrante

For Lisa Siobhan, Siraj Sandino, Durga Polashi and Willis

CHAPTER ONE

Bone Crunch

I went up the stairs, all three floors, slowly. My palm slid up on the curved and recessed mahogany bannister. As I turned the corner of the last flight, my heart stopped. I noticed a light bioscoping out through the keyhole in my apartment door. My palm gripped the bannister. My insides lit up. A stimulus of sorts that combines chill with warmth, the knee-weakening urgency. I could describe it in so many ways. Hormones zipped by, like Formula One cars on the hairpin turns of L'île Notre-Dame. Then the light was gone. I was hopeful that Myra had reached home before me and had decided on a surprise, probably something totally crazy! I went slowly up to the door. No noise. I was going to turn the tables on her. Yes! The door was open.

I pushed it open and stuck my hand slowly into the dark gap, to turn on the lights. I had just about reached the tip of the switch when a dry, parched, callused hand grabbed my wrist and wrenched me in and my face hit the door frame on the left-hand side of my forehead, above the eye. I stumbled in and only had time to say "Myra?" Red was already dripping down my temple. Then something very heavy landed on my head. As I fell to the floor, my neck to the side, the room circled and I saw two guys standing over me with what looked like large padded baseball bats. One of them was young and the other was heavy-set. They were both grunting. The younger fellow had a Cantinflas look on his face. As I lay on the ground, lifting my hands up tentatively, with them towering above me, I felt a steel-toed boot plunge into my stomach, then another penetrated my ribs. I heard the bones crunch inwards like a rattan chair giving way. I felt my lungs were now incomplete. Non-functional.

I must have passed out, because I don't remember squat about anything after that.

My landlord found me at midnight in a mound of freshly piled snow, about eighty centimetres high, at the bottom of the fire escape behind my kitchen. There were multiple fractures to my legs. Several bones in my collar and ribs had cracked. My jaw and both of my hands had also been broken. It was the depth of the recently fallen snow that had astonishingly saved my life. Nothing had broken open my skull or penetrated my heart. I had committed suicide, they decided.

When I awoke, I figured I was strung up, my whole head bandaged and no sign of Myra. I could make sounds through swollen lips, but I didn't know what I was saying. I was making liquid noises as the shapes in the room morphed around me like globules in pink and blue. I saw the map of the African continent distended on the ceiling, like rubber mats, down the walls. Like plastic paint that had dried. I think I said Sierra Leone or Congo repeatedly, for no reason, but the specific word didn't actually matter. Or maybe I said Côte d'Ivoire or Leon Spinks, Maradona or Kunta Kinte or rubber, robber or leather, lather, diamond and also strangely, enough, Finkelstein, which came out as Ficklestheeen— whatever was easier to push out of my mouth. I was gurgling out a strange language, a vocabulary that meant something to me, and I was engrossed in the way that I could swish the words around in my mouth, like mouthwash, and then release them from the peculiarity of the sounds, themselves. Motor neurons inside my mouth were propelling unheard-of phrases with my suddenly acquired acumen and fluidity in political geography, linguistics and sports heroes.

At some point Myra's face appeared above the little hole through which I could see. She had tears and a smile. I knew then that I had survived and was in good hands. The globules were actually nurses milling around. Their voices sounded like those of nuns in a monastery. The lights in the room flickered like candles in a cloister. Myra brought her lips close to my pouted arse-hole-shaped mouth and repeated Royal Vic! Royal Vic! I became totally aware. I was in the same blessed hospital in which I had been born. I was reminded of the picture of my father holding me wrapped in a white towel, a few seconds after my mum popped me out. I had made a lot of noise then, too, or so they tell me. And then I was put in a warm incubator bed, as I was born a blue baby.

I looked around and saw what I thought were prisoners, lined up against the wall. Waving, smiling from a distance. Family.

Myra, her father, my parents and grandparents were all there. I had a nose tube that whispered cold oxygen into my lungs and then on to my mixed-race brains. On either side of my bed were green and blue monitors on which healthy sine waves sauntered by. I saw everything through a monocular device that some kind nurse had enabled for me, over my left eye. My mouth was also surrounded by a bandage, like in a kind of pouch.

Myra sat close and said, "Don't say a word, babe. You were not trying to kill yourself. Okay? We know that. Don't say a word." Sierra Leone I said, Sierra Leone. That stayed in my head. Then Myra's father whispered into my ear, "Break and enter. That's our story. Break and enter. Get well, buddy. There's a lot to do." And recover I did. Like a bolt from the skies, that comes down like a zig-zag in cartoons. Every day, one bandage went out and so did my infatuation with Africa, sliding down the ceiling to the fluorescent-lit wall; boxers kept drifting away, Finkelstein, nuns, candles were all slowly gone.

For the next seven days, Myra rarely left the hospital. When she did, however briefly, she ensured her father was sitting next to me. My grandfather, RK, came nearly every day, as did my parents. My father and mother alternated evenings. My bed was often surrounded, as if somehow the family had sensed it was necessary to encircle me. Myra's dad assumed direction; he wrote down schedules and organized what can only be called a vigil. I made a few feeble protests, wanting to be alone, but they thought a twenty-four-hour presence was a better idea.

I was told that the police were preparing to question me. Apparently, they believed my much-too-eager landlord, who had spread the word that I had tried to kill myself by jumping off the fire escape, because I had recently been fired from my job. I tried to make it adamantly clear that I hadn't jumped and didn't want to die.

I awoke one morning to see Mrs. Meeropol standing at the foot of my bed. For a moment, I thought she was standing at the top of the stairs, impatient for a long discussion and ready to make tea. She came around the top and pressed her palm to my forehead. "I've heard about your alleged jump. I don't believe it. I told Nat and he says he's thinking of you all the time."

I accepted Gerry's proposed idea of a break and enter. All we had to do was state that some money and a watch were missing. So, the story came out that I had resisted a break-in with such courage and dexterity that the robbers had thrown me down the fire escape in a state of induced terror. I liked that story.

For the first time, I noticed that Myra's dad was actually a stocky fellow. While everyone was busy I motioned him aside and tried to tell him through my pouted lips that he'd find the scribbled pages with the suspect's handwriting in my pant pocket. Suspect. The Lady. The Gestapo chief. He clearly understood, even though I wasn't sure I was making any sense. He nodded and replied, "I have it already and her i's match. She makes a circle instead of a dot. It's her all right." Fuckin-A! He was quick, that guy, making it into my pockets before the cops. Maybe Myra had told him where to look.

I felt enormously relieved that the evidence I had so painfully gathered was safe and in good hands. I immediately demanded a dose of "porphine," that mind-bending drug made from poppies growing in the blue-green hills of Afghanistan. How Kandahar was indeed marshalling every move. The nurse prodded the syringe into a Y-tube next to the bag of dextrose draining into my veins. Before the lights went out, Myra said, "Babe, we're gonna assault their head-quarters. It's gonna be war!"

The pain disappeared for six or seven hours. The war lingered on. I again demanded the "porphine" though my muzzled mouth. The nurse, an elderly Barbadian woman, told me, "Honee dear, now you don't hesitate to ask for pain killahs! Ras! Anytime!"

"Yes, ma'am," I concurred silently.

I had lots of time to think, although it may not have always been coherent. I wondered why Corinthe had put together a hit team to take me out only a few months after I had joined the company. Why was she panicking?

She needn't have worried—I wasn't about to tell the cops anything. They came and dutifully asked me questions for about two hours. They wanted to know if I could recognize anyone from a file of pictures they had brought with them. I didn't see anyone even vaguely resembling the out-of-focus images I had of my assailants. Then they wanted to know if I had ever received or bought stolen goods. That amused me, but it hurt too much to smile, so I just swayed my head from side to side. They smiled and winked because they had seen Russell Peters do the Asian bobbing head thing at the Bell Centre. They eventually thanked me for my time and left, mighty pleased.

My mother made a habit of sitting next to my bed. She gently ran her hands over my chest while tears rolled down her cheeks. She'd do that while my grandmother prowled outside the room in a new pair of sneakers and grossly out-of-style Sears slacks, monitoring the corridor as if ready to kick-box any unwanted intruder.

I was simultaneously in pain and happy. For once I felt my life had meaning; that the people I loved had come together. There was, for the first time, a collective action being undertaken by the whole family. The people who were dear to me were like warm candles glowing inside. I don't mean anything religious, other than that I felt their illuminating presence inside me, and the origin of their light lay in each of them. Finally, I had begun to discover what I could do and not simply be an observer.

I was in the hospital almost six weeks. They moved me to a single room for the last two even though I didn't have the insurance to cover it. I was grateful to Myra's dad, Mr. Banks. Afterwards, I was sent home with instructions to follow the rehabilitation program administered in a community centre in Notre Dame de Grâce. The local clinic assigned a nurse to me for weekly check-ups.

My new place of residence was a super-secret apartment along the southern edges of the city near my grandparents' condo, and it was announced to friends and anyone else who asked that I was recuperating in Florida. My personal insurance and the Quebec Provincial Insurance had come through with a modest compensation package, including assistance for victims of crime. I was to get a yet-to-be-determined lump sum along with one thousand dollars a month.

Myra had packed all my belongings, closed out my apartment, then closed out hers as well before moving in. Nobody other than immediate family and the Health Services knew where we were staying. We were now far from the Main. Something about that dimly registered in my mind, but I suppose all enigmas fade eventually, and you can't salvage what no longer exists. Even though I doubt she would ever leave the Main, Mrs. Meeropol would understand that thought.

I wanted to visit her as soon as I could. I felt badly that I had left her in the dark. She suffered silently. It was the fog. The pall that hung down low, the stories of wave upon wave of migrating nomads, settling and then moving on, opening stores and closing, dogs that stayed unleashed or remained tethered, business that brought in monthly family income and had their dreams destroyed in no time, poets and performers who carved their presence with initials on polished bar tables and then moved to LA. at the first opportunity. Indecision about staying, taking sides or wading in. The wringing of the hands in sadness and anger. The elusiveness of being away and being at home. The fog of being at war— being involved without conviction.

As in the hospital, my mother came to sit and run her hands gently over my chest. I've learned that is what mothers do: sit by you and comfort you and watch out for you. Every day she brought a dish she had made. As my jaws attained greater amplitude and wavelength, she introduced meats. I was definitely requiring proteins, she said.

After another month, my plasters were removed at the community clinic. I didn't require surgery on either my legs or my face. The ribs, too, were healing on their own. In fact, after only two months I was able to limp around the apartment and begin physio. Myra bought a small second-hand car to help get me there. I found out later that my parents had helped her with it.

During the long afternoons, I stared at the ceiling. Gazing up, I gradually recovered the image of the thin, hideous-looking guy I had first seen against the ceiling hovering over me and pounding away. Cantinflas. There was something unique about that Mexican actor I couldn't quite define, but his dark outline became clearer and clearer each time he landed a blow. It was strange; I'd raise my hands in a protective gesture while the blow came closer and closer, like in a slow-motion sequence. At some point, as I played that memory back and forth in my mind, I finally realized he had a missing section to his lower lip. That was it! Yes, I remembered his lower lip was cut and kind of tucked in on one side, like a section had been sliced away.

My grandfather, RK, was a great sketcher and he tried, based on my increasingly accurate descriptions, to capture the likeness of the thug who had busted me up. Finally, he achieved it, a wonderful composite that the Montreal Police would never see. Gerry Banks did, and so did Myra; they both studied it before they began to look for him.

CHAPTER TWO

Debris from the Skies

There were two incidents. In mid-air, as it were. Without warning. Several years apart. Incomprehensible, but inextricably associated. Like two howitzers launched from the same pod in different directions. Leaving a trail behind that drifted together.

First, there was the plane crash, several years ago. Debris fell from the sky and spread in a lazy descent over the acquiescent countryside. A freak encounter with Myra, under most peculiar circumstances, introduced me to the story of this crash that happened several years ago in northern Quebec. "A small plane only," she had informed me, with her bristling brown eyebrows raised in a distracted manner. "But, deep stuff! Big with implications." I knew nothing about it. A well-known painter had been blown to bits, she added. Minor parts of the plane were retrieved and an investigation was carried out, but it was never established why the plane had gone down. It was proposed that it could have been engine failure or an unusual wind, or both, and the case had been closed. Strange indeed, she had asserted. But there was more to come.

Now, the second incident.

He was dissected by a missile from a drone, today's eliminator of choice. Erased. My one friend from kindergarten on.

It was not on the news. The email arrived the next morning addressed to me. His mother stood at the top of the stairs in silence, wrapped in her old red shawl. I went up the stairs, my left knee grazing the wall. Mrs. Meeropol put her arms out feebly. I put my arms around her and for the first time we embraced. Dust, bones, fascia, steel parts, charred skin had been deeply implanted in a small crater on a mountain pass, where Christiane Amanpour had left her CNN mark with her O-sounding inflection on every word she used. Bora! Bora! She said with a felicific howl. A thousand arcing curves of GI piss had been jeeringly deposited on the holy book of a religion. The absurdity of a new generation of airborne freedom fighters, bounty hunters for democracy, had become the order of the day.

With the plane crash story, a seed had been sown. A plant would grow. Perhaps an unknown fruit or flower would result.

Of course, small planes do come down once in a while. But my new acquaintance felt, although she could not prove it, that the crash was an act of sabotage, a murder plot. She felt she knew too much. Her brown eyes looked far away and her casual intensity gripped me. It was while struggling with this incident that the unexpected and startling began to unfold.

My grandfather, whom I informed about the plane crash situation and who was prone to drawing outsized conclusions from small observations, and Mrs. Meeropol, a lonely woman with a proclivity towards reminiscing, were both convinced that I was now well on my way to solving the roots of iniquity, alienability, and the specific impunity enjoyed by a certain crust of society from criminal prosecution.

He lit his pipe, wagged his finger and said, "When you have eliminated the impossible, whatever remains, however improbable, must be the truth." A quote memorized from Arthur Conan Doyle. Puffs of scented clouds rose above my grandfather's satisfied smile. I knew then that without a visit to the scene of the crime, the wisdom of my grandfather would remain just what it was.

I read as voraciously as I could, from my teenage years. Egged on by RK, of course. He finished a book and handed it to me. Short stories; Marquez, Camus, Tagore, Joyce, Dickens, Wilde, Manto, Twain, even some Sartre and contemporary whodunits, as well. In no order and with no plan. Then I started reading the Russian greats. Some Pushkin, Turgenev, Dostoevsky, Gorky. I never tried to find literary merit, only the unfolding of a story. Documenting a time and class belittlement in that period. Suffering, exile, escapade and perpetuating memory, just documenting. Bewildered often, by intrigue and desperate lives unfolding. I did not quite understand that there could be a philosophy behind every story, every act of intrigue or jealousy, that there was an urge to address not just unfairness and evil, but the logic behind evil. Then I read Gogol and the Diary of a Madman. It was transformative. You can go mad, suffering mentally and not doing anything or at least you will be certified as such, if you only absorb and do not wring out the sponge in your head and let every drop of filth and accumulated bilious scum that the sponge picks up; and there is rancid oil and water, fungus and particles of dirt, miscible or not, drop on the floor. Then what do you do? Mop it and move on? Do you go home, lie down and die?

Trois-Pistoles

Nothing happens here. Absolutely nothing. Puffs of hot condensed air mixed with steam spurt from the side vents of brick houses like smoke signals and dissipate before they reach the rooftops. The skies are bloodless. The woeful horn of a ferry cuts through the air as the bow slices through the waves every hour of every day from 7 a.m. to 7 p.m., struggling from Rivière-du-Loup to Saint-Siméon. Subdued exchanges in the village mimic the chatter of burbling streams running behind the cottages. Tawny-faced farmers, of mixed Indigenous and European heritage, retired and relaxed, slow down to greet each other. Their lower jaws jut out, accompanied by the clicking sounds of unhinged dentures moulded with imprecise impressions.

Twice a day the steady hum of a prop plane is heard somewhere in the southwest skies. Delivering bargain mail-order shopping inducements or parsimonious gifts from relatives who left town long ago. On the ground, mischievous white-tailed deer appear around backyards sneering at dazed out-of-season hunters. Through the kitchen windows, large antlered moose appear; the hunter munches quickly on chips, wipes the beer foam from his moustache, swears incoherently under his poo-breath, and rushes out. They all look like Maxim Gorkys around here.

People in Trois-Pistoles like getting mail, be it the cards from Acadian cousins who have moved to Lake Charles, Louisiana to revive *le français québécois*, or the Valentine greetings from an Irish Catholic nun to her housebound lesbian sister.

Emil Leblanc's calf muscles tighten and relax as he strides past each home. He wears his regulation dark blue uniform, navy blue mailbag slung across his shoulder, and he carries a pile of letters, envelopes, and flyers between his fingers. As he sorts he hums, then takes a shortcut across the gravel path to the mailbox next door. Further down the street an old man with a leather apron around his waist steps out of a crawl space, pulls up his overalls, and climbs the stairs to the house. A band of children rush at each other in a grassy plot behind a raised mound and then wave at Emil who waves back, as he always does.

The small Piper airplane takes a large parabolic curve high over the northern edge of the city. Linda St-Onge sits in the front row. She took philosophy in college and taught geometry in high school before committing to painting. On her canvases geometric shapes, tall structures, and cityscapes soar upwards before being interrupted abruptly with rain showers, snowstorms, and terrifying storm clouds. Obelisks rise and spear the sky and lightning strikes back in reprisal. Whatever rises up assertively receives an unambiguous response from the angry skies. And debris falls.

The Rivière-du-Loup ground control tells the pilot to circle for a few more minutes. Normally the plane would have been instructed to come in directly from the south and land, but another small plane, late to leave for its destination, is now taking off.

Linda looks out through the window and can see the tiresome green farmland below, the undecided sunlight reflecting off the blue-green river. She has taken this flight at least a dozen times. She applies some lipstick to her faintly quivering lips and then folds her purse. Red on pale.

She is not going to make it easy for them. She is not the one who engaged in subterfuge and cruel secrets. She has done nothing wrong.

A parabola is formed by the intersection of a uniform symmetric cone by a flat plane at an angle. The points of intersection are critical. Fragility and resentment can cut it open and lay it bare.

It is 11:30 in the morning when Emil Leblanc hears the parabola being sliced out of the cone in the sky. It is like a crack followed by a thunderclap and then a ringing boom. He looks up and can't see anything. The sky is clear. He can only hear the sound reverberating in his ears. "What the hell was that?"

He turns a full three hundred and sixty degrees. The children in the distance have stopped playing and are also looking up. The Gorky with the leather apron steps out of his door to scan the skies. Another Gorky steps onto his patio and looks up. But there is nothing to be seen.

The children begin again to chase each other in disharmonious circles.

Far away down in the valley the river loops back upon itself, glittering in the sunlight. The sound, however, continues to play on his mind. Something has gone awry. A sunny day has been pierced and drenched in red blood cells. He carries on delivering the mail but keeps looking up. Somewhere in the distance, debris has started to descend, unseen. Fragments. Shattered pieces of life and love. Jealousy, carnal minutiae, torn knee joints and horn-rimmed spectacles with eyelids thermally attached along with engine parts, titanium shields, and annealed aluminum alloy shimmer in the convective current under the bright sunlight. Over a surprisingly wide swath of country they spread, tumbling down in a non-aerodynamic descent, slowly flipping over and over.

In the afternoon, as he passes by the church, the toothless Gorky carpenter repairing the wooden frames of the stained-glass windows asks, "Hey! Emil! *Tabarnac! As-tu entendu?* The plane crash? No?" Emil looks up again. His shoulders droop. Of course, the plane from Montreal.

CHAPTER THREE

Diamond Dust

I had been keeping a daily journal. A simple project about the neighbourhood peppered with sufficient inaccuracies and digressions to ultimately morph into a work of fiction. Both tulips and weeds grew out of the ground at the turn of a losing battle for real summer. I shared segments with the totally charismatic Mrs. Meeropol, her son—my unfaltering high school and neighbourhood friend Nat, and, at times, my unfathomable grandfather RK. While RK nodded, his eyebrows flaring, Mrs. Meeropol wrung her fingers with expectation, interrupting me with related stories she thought I ought to know. Nat was curious but mostly distracted. Sadly. I confess that nothing remotely fascinating happened in my life or in my diary until this woman sauntered in and uncovered the plane crash story to me. She ran a rake through my indifferent soil. Sun and rain did what they do and leaves and petals opened, vermin crawled, worms multiplied, bushes bloomed, diseases festered, and acid fell from the skies. My diary grew, stalled, wilted, changed direction, and then slowly evolved into an uninterruptable storm, a tsunami that transformed my life. My friendship with Nat was integral to my neighbourhood notes.

My part-time job as a desk clerk at a courier company was inadequate to pay my bills or my frequent sojourns to watering holes on that stretch. Nat and I had established key observation posts in several of these, from where we would scan and sneer at total unknowns or cajole the regulars. He held court. I marvelled at his ability to practice a kind of brinkmanship, taking things to an edge in terms of provocations and then settling down to making new friends or forever dismissing the rest as "bozos." And then there was the flashy sexuality. Real and imaginary carnal forays in dim apartments, knees pushing against groins, wharfs sliding into lakes, and teeth biting into tanned shoulders. All this was duly entered in the journal. He did things, I recorded them. I did not do much, on my own. Just a little perhaps. I imagined a lot. Let's put it that way. Now, what chance made me meet Myra, this bushy eye-browed woman, who casually informed me about the unsolved plane crash and disappeared for long periods? I would say that she found me, like when you are in a séance and you call up a medium. I became the medium.

I found a second part-time job that required I watch television in the evenings. They had given me a device with an encoder to record which channels I visited and for how long. I didn't have to punch any buttons; I was simply required to wear it on my belt. I hadn't told the company during the interview that I only owned a small Zenith that barely managed occasional grey and grainy images, so I made the investment and bought a new second-hand TV. Then, while single-handedly trying to carry it to my apartment, I threw out my back.

The pain started slowly but by the next morning I was barely able to roll out of bed. I spent two days either lying down or on hands and knees crawling between microwave and bed, heating up a magic beanbag for the small of my back. It would relieve the pain for about ten minutes before the excruciating contraction returned. Like a hydraulic tong, it forced me to arch my torso and scream my surrender. I spent a full hour in the bathtub and foolishly thought that the contraction had left. It snapped back as soon as I tried to towel.

So, on the third day, despite a deep suspicion of chiropractors, I took the advice of Nat and visited a practice close to my apartment. With hands on hips and knees bent I hobbled across Boulevard St-Laurent. My boss at work had understood my absence because she suffered from bouts of spondylitis. She made a remark, too coyly for my liking, about *what exactly* I had been doing, *Que faisiez-vous, jeune homme? Peut-être je ne veux pas savoir!*

There was a painting of New York City in winter, done in oil, hanging in the lobby just outside the door to the doctor's examination room. I was immediately taken in. The snow drifted down in a remarkably separate dimension. I looked at it and felt I could catch the flakes if I put out my hand. Some artists dab paint on the canvas to signify falling snow. Doesn't work for me. This artist had somehow imparted a subdued and effective sparkle above a dark, bustling street. I wanted to sit down and stare at it. But of course, I couldn't sit and this was not a museum.

She was the receptionist who sat behind a semi-circular counter and chatted away on the phone with a thousand you-know-what-I-means interspersed with emphatic sighs of frustration and disgust. Her tinny voice scratched my eardrums like nails on a blackboard and her mispronounced consonants irritated me. She finally hung up and asked if I would like to sit, seeing as my appointment wasn't for another fifteen minutes. I promptly advised her that the only reason I was there was because I couldn't sit without being in great pain.

"Oh!" She replied nonchalantly and carried on chewing her gum, adding a slapping sound to the previous swishing sound. I stared at her over the top of my glasses. She put her head down. I looked away and tried to focus on the painting. This happened again, before she said, "I see that you like something about that painting."

"Uh-huh, I do." I looked at her face more carefully. Very pleasant, actually.

Sensing my approval, she jutted her chin out in a playful way. "Well, there's a long history to that painting and the doctor might tell you if you ask him." She smiled before going back to slapping gum.

Dr. Roberge opened his door at exactly the appointed time and waved me in. A tall man with large hands, he wore a striped t-shirt and loose slacks. His sneakers had Nike bottoms on designer leather uppers. They made no noise. He had one eyebrow raised and took a quick look at the receptionist. She put her head down. I was irritated by the fact that there had been no previous patient and he could easily have taken me earlier. He did not ask any questions, as he had clearly leafed through what I had filled out. It was lying on his desk. He had me take off my shirt and asked me to lie down on my stomach and then measured my back with his fingers. He made strange flicks with his fingers at the end of certain manoeuvres. I didn't know what he was doing, but he was definitely into his technique. After about ten minutes, he asked me to lie on my back and then he positioned himself behind me. He started stretching my neck very slowly. It felt good. I felt the relief I had come for. The tension was dissolving.

When he finished I simply walked outside to make the payment with the money earned from my new job, noting that so far, I had worked for free, given the cost of the TV and the visit to the chiropractor. The receptionist asked if I had mentioned the painting.

"No, I didn't, but if you know about it why don't you tell me?" I said it aggressively, although that didn't seem to register on her. She casually licked the pen and thought it over.

"You're the only one who has really looked at the painting in my two years here. I'm off in five minutes. You can meet me at the corner café, if you want, and I'll tell you."

I liked the painting. It was a work of art. It should have been in a private home or a museum. In this lobby on an unlit wall seemed the wrong place for it. And besides, this was definitely shaping up to be a potential diary entry. "Okay! I'll see you in five minutes."

I hobbled across the street and sat down at the café next to the large windows. I ordered a cappuccino and sipped it very slowly. Five minutes passed and she had not appeared. Five minutes turned to twenty and she still hadn't turned up. At this point I felt like I wanted to yell at her: she had stood me up. I slowly crossed the street and climbed the stairs painfully to the doctor's office. The door was ajar.

As soon as I re-entered the lobby I knew something was wrong. I heard her whimpering from inside the doctor's room, "I didn't mean to! I didn't mean to!" And to my amazement, I noticed the painting was gone from the wall.

I made a coughing sound and heard the shuffle of feet behind the doctor's door. He eased himself out and then closed the door behind him before demanding, "Yes?"

"Sorry to bother you . . . I was supposed to meet your receptionist for coffee downstairs." Awkwardness shrinks my newly stretched spinal column.

"She's gone for the day." He said briskly.

I walked away. I simply went down the stairs and walked home, knowing she was still in there with him. But it troubled me. Why had he not acknowledged her presence? Why had the painting disappeared? And why had I been treated like riff-raff?

I entered my apartment, found my encoder, and turned on the TV. The device started to change lights and flicker. I pulled out my diary and began to record the event, with appropriate embellishments. I was pretty sure I'd run into her again, so I noted that, too. This was to be a turning point.

Then about three months later, when the snow had melted, I was back from my day job at the courier company and enjoying a large sticky Danish at the same café when she walked in. The gum-slapping garrulousness was gone. Her hair was loose and in disarray, no longer tied in the tight bun I remembered. She looked haggard.

She saw me and her hand quickly went to her face but it was too late, our eyes had met. I waved to her. She peered at me carefully, as if trying to recognize who I might be. She followed that with a startled look and then, smiling, walked over to my table and said, "Hi! How are ya?" I realized then how good an act she can put on. "How's your back?"

"Recovered. Nice of you to remember."

I didn't tell her that she might be considered gorgeous, despite the tornado-hit looks. Instead I said, "I've never been back to the doctor."

"Good for you. I quit right after."

"Are you working somewhere else?"

"Sort of."

I asked if I could offer her a coffee and went up to the counter to do so. Awkwardness put aside. When I returned, I noticed her stockings had a long run shaped like Italy working its way down the inside of her leg.

Without any prodding, she immediately started to chat. "That painting. Did you notice the sparkle in it?"

I said that I had, of course.

"Well, it's one of those things. You know what I mean? Very subtle. You wanna talk about it?" She sipped her coffee and raised her eyebrows. She spoke like a bougainvillea plant would. Sprightly petals and wilted leaves. Reticent and sensitive with thorn on the branches. She took another sip. "Once I noticed that, too, you know, so I asked him what was in the paint. And he said 'diamonds, my dear, diamonds,' in an off-handed way, but then he obviously regretted having said it because he added he was just kidding."

Diamond dust! And that's why he didn't have any lights shining on it. It made it too obvious. She looked into my eyes and I could see she was searching for some recognition.

The snow seemed to have a life of its own. Her eyebrows had lifted and her mouth was partly opened. For a moment, I felt the flakes coming down my entire body, condensing into droplets of moisture that flowed down ridges in my torso.

"I knew you had noticed. You can tell when a person's got it." Her confidence had returned. She asserted that the doctor was a strange man. That he hauled her into his office after I had left and gave her the third degree. She was scolded for mentioning the painting! She confirmed she was still there when I went back. You know!

I enjoyed her gathering energy. I told her I heard her protesting. I knew something was wrong and I didn't like it. But I had no reason to stay. To be honest, I told her, I was upset she hadn't shown up to have coffee as she had agreed. "I'm glad to meet you again after so many months."

"Same here! Same here!" She put her palm on the back of my hand and looked at me again with questioning eyes. "You thought I was an idiot, right? Like the way I just walked away from a promise. I was mad, ready to quit on him. You don't think I'm an idiot, do you? By the way, my name is Myra, Myra Banks."

"I'm Chuck," I replied, putting my other hand on top of hers. It felt warm.

She told me that he had given her the pink slip when she went to work the next day.

"Arse-hole! But I wanted to quit anyway."

"I'm sorry. I guess I was partly responsible."

"Oh! It's nothing. Life goes on." She was silent for a while, looking out at the cars and the people in the street.

I asked if she remembered the name of the artist. I was trying to get her attention.

"Yes. She signs *L. St-Onge*. Her first name was Linda. She was his wife. She died in a plane crash in Trois-Pistoles while he was having an affair with a lady he later married. I guess that's another story."

"What do you mean?"

She looked out to the street again, looked back at me and then got up and said, "Gotta go. Got an audition and then classes."

She thanked me for the coffee and left like a gust of wind. I never got to ask her what audition, what classes? I saw her cross the street briskly with her head down.

The next day I remembered her lips teasing the edge of the coffee cup. I remembered, too, her legs as she crossed the street. I saw them as the choreographed footwork of a dancer on a darkened stage, a follow spot trained from the hips down to the arched heels. I saw again the rip in her stockings, and behind it all, diffused and sparkling, the snow fell gradually.

Even though I had originally been irritated at her masticating, casual persona, a change had now taken place. Removed from the receptionist's desk, she seemed distressed, less snappy and cocksure. A withdrawn distraction seemed to glow in her eyes.

I took to parking myself in the same café where we had met, taking the same seat beside the same window. It was like I was on a cliff top overlooking an undulating valley. My insides groaned and knocked around like the clanging of a lonesome broken gate on a windy promontory. *Trois-Pistoles.* I waited. Would she sneak in from behind and put her arm on my shoulder? Would she sit next to me as I quietly added to my diary?

My expectations had been founded on a single chance encounter. I realized I needed to discuss this with Nat, or perhaps his mother—and, if necessary, my grandfather. The plane crash story was way too much to keep concealed.

CHAPTER FOUR

Broken China

After hearing the Trois-Pistoles story, I felt unnervingly implicated, intrinsically culpable. It was the kind of story that triggers benign fidgety violence. I kept pumping staples into the air, and into the window next to my desk with a desktop stapler. The anxiousness of expecting an unbearable outcome, that could be both life-changing and yet tear things apart. I went to the courier company for several weeks somewhat bothered. I was unable and incapable of figuring out where I had previously run into the name *Trois-Pistoles* before.

On a Wednesday morning, a grey Mercedes-Benz pulled up and parked itself outside my office window. The driver left the car running as he walked across to an adjoining office. There was nothing to it, except the Benz kept idling outside, the clanging of its diesel engine penetrating through the glass. I looked at it a few times and was convinced that I was remembering a scene from a haunting film from the past that was re-enacting itself again. In that film or an advertisement, perhaps, a woman had jumped out after parking a Mercedes on a hilltop on a foggy morning. She clutched her coat while she held onto a box and the wind blew her hair into long curls. She dropped the box into a hole and started kicking dirt into it, with her high heels, to cover it up. Cover-up. The box.

Then this man at my courier office returned to the car and suddenly, everything came back to me. Like a detonation. I knew where I had run into Trois-Pistoles.

Several years ago, a lady wearing a rather outsized pair of dark glasses, a long parka-style coat, and a long necklace bouncing against her soft contoured chest had walked in after parking her Mercedes. I remembered the diesel engine idling outside then, too. She came saying she had a package to be delivered to a town in the Bas-St-Laurent, the region located along the south shore of the river east of Quebec City. I was an apprentice at the time, learning the trade, anxious to please. I remembered her being cautious as she carefully put the package on the counter, and yet in a terrible hurry as she filled out the waybill. She insisted it be put on the flight the next morning. Trois-Pistoles!

"And not on any other," she distinctly said. "I need it to get there tomorrow morning. Okay?" Said with Teutonic belligerence.

I told her I understood the urgency and assured her it would be on the right flight. Without exception. Besides, there was only one flight each day to Rivière-du-Loup, the airport closest to the town of Trois-Pistoles, where the package was addressed.

She kept looking at her Mercedes-Benz, which she had left running, as if drawing strength from the sound of its presence. And then she left.

The next morning, I rifled through the archives at the back for the waybill slips from years ago. I eventually confirmed that, indeed, on June 16 of 1998, I had sent a package to be delivered to Trois-Pistoles on the next day's flight. *Je suis complice.* I stepped out and was confronted by a swift slap to the face. The howling wind ensured that I understood that.

I made my way to the Sherbrooke Street city library, shivering in the spring haze. When I crossed the six lanes on Sherbrooke, I felt I had walked over water, hot coal, ice, and a mudslide that kept sucking at my feet like I would never make it across. The pedestrian sign still said there were fifteen seconds left and yet every step swallowed up many more seconds than I thought it should. I found the newspapers for that day and the following week and looked through them with fingers that quaked on their own. I discovered from the June 19 news report that not only had Linda St-Onge died in an airplane crash two days prior, but that her body, as well as those of the two pilots and others in the plane had not been recovered. Not a trace, not a memory, not a protest, not a poem, nor an insurrection had happened. Elimination with extreme prejudice. Obliteration.

There were unverified reports that local villagers had heard a sound and seen the plane on fire. The RCMP had taken up the case.

As I continued the research, I learned that the case was very quickly closed shut, cold. Eventually I discovered a short summary of a final report that suggested that the plane had been caught in a freak crosswind which flipped it over prior to its descent into the water. While some parts of the plane had been retrieved, the exact cause of the crash would probably never be known.

At the end of that week of anxiety and regret, I decided to revisit the sombre Dr. Roberge. On arriving at his office, walking as if again in pain, I was told that he had recently sold the practice to a younger doctor. I acted shocked by the news and asked the receptionist where the good man could be found, as I truly appreciated the help he had been to me. She immediately suggested that I see the new chiropractor. I sighed and said I would think it over and asked again where Dr. Roberge might be.

"In the Bahamas," she answered. "He and his wife moved there. It's not as if they don't have the money."

"He got married?" I exclaimed.

"Years ago," she laughed at my foolish query. "To one of the Gabriel-Jacops."

"Ah," I said, as if the name meant something to me. "Gabriel-Jacops. Of course, I knew that."

"Good-day, Mr. Bhatt. Should your pain continue, do consider the services of the new doctor." My pain? Right! My pain.

I looked at her compounded face with its professional demeanour. She did not chew gum, nor talk incessantly on the phone, nor ignore her client. She showed, I thought, an annoying lack of tempestuousness. I was comparing.

A newspaper from the Bas-St-Laurent stated that the Jacops Foundation had sponsored a show in Montreal of the works of Linda St-Onge in which she had integrated diamond powder paste donated by the same foundation. The paintings, completed in her Trois-Pistoles studio, had been auctioned off and fetched a handsome sum for several charitable donations.

The unplanned encounter between the rich divorcée and the sophisticated chiropractor in a vernissage under helium lights, the casual greetings and exchanges of smiles at a black tie gathering organized for charity, the problems expressed about a strained pampered lumbar, the appointment made to try to fix the problem, the strong hands in the right place. To fix the problem. When had Linda actually found out?

I went back to the archives and again sorted through the waybills. The name of that lady in the Mercedes-Benz was *Mary Salvaggio*. Of course, not the name I had expected. But, of course. Nor had there been any closed-circuit security TV at the time of the transaction. She had stated in the form that the contents of the package were dried flowers. I made photocopies of all the evidence I had.

I found him standing near the front of the gates to his father's business, his head to one side, his shirt hanging below his denim jacket. The new street lamps on St-Laurent silhouetted him like a character out of The Big Combo. Noire gem. The temperature had fallen. Steam rising from the manholes added greyness. The lamplight bounced off the steam as it moved away in a slow drift towards the south. Nat looked down at the pavement, a cigarette hanging loose from his lips.

He didn't look good. His father—and his father before him—had been running the Meeropol tombstone business for over a hundred years. It was situated squat in the centre of the Main. Two weeks prior, Mr. Meeropol had gripped his chest and slowly collapsed on the pavement. For a while no one had noticed, because there was a car right in front of him and hardly anyone was on the sidewalk. By the time an ambulance was called, he was long gone. Nat Meeropol was informed while he was in New York waiting for an audition for a role in a movie. He rushed back immediately to Montreal, and for the first time in his life, became directly involved in the family business.

We had gone to school together at West End High and had never fallen out of touch. He'd come to my parents' downtown apartment and my grandfather, who was into names, jokingly referred to him as Nathuram, Mahatma Gandhi's killer. I'm not sure that went down too well with Nat when I explained to him that Nathuram Godse belonged to the Nazi-like extremist Hindu nationalist party at the time of the great partition of India. Nat, in turn, took jabs at my grandfather by calling him Biswas for no reason at all other than it being the only Indian name he could remember, having once read Naipaul.

Nat travelled to New York to improve his chances as an actor, but returned to Montreal as often as he left. Every time he came back we'd sit at a St-Laurent deli and devour a mountain of smoked meat on thin slices of rye. He'd be wiping mustard from his chin and complaining loudly about "outertowners," meaning folks from the suburbs who lined up noisily on the weekends as if on some cultural outing. Nat provoked people for no reason or at the slightest pretext. I'd control him as best I could, and then we'd walk up to a coffee shop to watch the people go by. He was exuberant, charming, and a roughneck and brawler when required. Hands and feet synchronized in style as he amused folks with cool greetings, a slap of the hands, a fist to the chest, and an exaggerated bow. All the establishments knew him. Some called him "Hollywood" but never to his face. I knew, because they'd refer to him as "Yer buddy, Mr. Hollywood," when I was on my own.

That was the pattern of our lives, summer and winter. The transitional seasons went by unnoticed, undocumented. But, I took notes.

When I saw him standing in front of the Meeropol Monument factory, I sensed the down in that sulking air. His eyes were red and he looked sideways when I called out from across the street. There were a bunch of fancy cars in front of an upscale restaurant, and he was looking bitterly at the valets who were getting into one car after another. They must have seen his father collapse but hadn't bothered. With their shades and white suits on, they had slid into car after car to drive them away to a parking lot on St-Dominique. Folks doing their job, like it was the most serious profession in the world. Yet on the sidewalk an old man, known to everyone in the neighbourhood, lay dying. I walked across and put my hands on his shoulders and he was a bit startled.

"Yo! Let's go for a drink, man!" he said, like I needed sympathy. We went to the Las Palmas. In the lighting that hung down over Boulevard St-Laurent his slouched walk accentuated his hurt. A fog hung low over the street.

"Remember the last time we were here and Martha Parizeau was there?" I said to distract him. Martha was a well-known dance critic, past her prime. She worked for one of the smaller tabloids.

"Yeah! That *kurva!* I don't see her writing much these days. Waz-up with her? She still around?" He seemed a bit more energized as he took a long slurp from his tall glass. *La Fin Du Monde.*

"You know, she had a daughter who tried acting for a while. You know where she is?" I knew he had known her.

"Yeah! Yeah! Sweet tight bitch!" He seemed to remember. His shoulders were rounded and he narrowed his eyes and pointed his fingers at me. He was remembering. He never took notes. He remembered. "Martha Parizeau was married to Gerry Banks, a broker. They had a cottage in the townships. But one of them was having fun on the fly and they broke up. So, the broker broke up! Hah! Hah! That was the last time she had a regular fuck. No fun since. She was never happy with any of the shows she reviewed. She trashed everything. Everyone was below her. She had trained with Merce Cunningham years ago. That was her only claim to whatever. Her daughter was Myra. Yeah, Myra Banks. Think she wanted to become an actor."

He said actorrrr in a derisive manner. I was annoyed.

"Ain't seen her in a while. Last time was in a St-Denis studio. Heard she worked as a clerk somewhere on the side and sometimes she just walks around in a daze. You know what I mean? Ah-hah! She'd be doing the gutter glitter and no one would know, man. She's goooouud." Slow, curled up consonants.

"Actually, she was working at the front desk of the chiro you sent me to, just there across the street. That's where I met her. Just so you know. And then she got fired, I think. She did seem a bit distracted." I looked curtly at him in the eye.

"No kidding! Oh! Yeah? How'd you know she was Martha's daughter?"

"You told me, Mr. Meeropol, when I mentioned her last time. You said she was strange."

"Oh! Did I? She and Martha didn't get along. Poor thing. She is cute, ya know!"

"Weird! Here's her mum, all stand-offish and super critical, no sex you say, and her kid goes all out?" I was probing him.

"Hold on! I didn't say she went all out, Chuck. That's not what I said. Maybe it's not the way it seems on the surface." He said this with great emphasis. "Like, I think she's had a plan to be an actor. She even tried singing. She dances well. Only sometimes she gets into a screwed-up mood; maybe walks around kind of lost and folks think she's turning tricks. But she's no hooker." I liked these sudden orbiting introspections in him. He hovered and then landed.

"I didn't say she was. Have you seen her lately?"

"Like my old man, you know. He never went out of his way to hustle for business. Folks came to him. You do what is natural. Know what I mean? She does what comes natural to her. And she don't care what the hood thinks. And that's pretty cool with me."

I hadn't been successful. I thought he was going to chat about his dad now. But he didn't.

"Yeah, actually she's quite a pleasant chick. Definitely friendly." He continued talking about her and I wanted to listen. I needed to hear what he had to say. My distraction was widespread and growing. I wanted to find Myra.

Bring her in. I needed her badly inside my head. There was a life force in her that surrounded me like cool water in a brook in a mountain pass somewhere in Armenia, or in the Caucuses, in Turkey on the Bosporus, or maybe in Kashmir or Azerbaijan, some distant place I had never been. My mind flapped its wings, like a gull careening from side to side, diving, swooping, and skimming the surface of water and earth as I tried to call her to me, but I couldn't bring her in. She flew by.

"And what's with you man! What's your story?" He said that with a weird smile, as if he was reading my thoughts.

And then I told Nat about the lady who had delivered the courier package to me, some twelve years ago, the day before an airplane crash. I filled in all the details and when I finished there was silence. He stared at me. He had come to a complete halt. And then!

Suddenly, "Fuck! That was an IED she handed to you, man! An IED! Like, are you joshing me or what?"

Everything in my life was connecting: Myra, the lady with the parcel, my chiro with the diamond dust painting, the plane crash. My life was connected to all of it and it was all disconnected as well and I needed him to understand. Nat was the only one I could connect with.

"I put it on the plane. I've hardly slept since." There was a long silence. He stared into my eyes. I could see a thin film of water accumulate around the edge of his eyes.

"It could have blown up right there, man!" His voice had weakened.

"Yeah, but it didn't."

He whispered softly, "Are you going to the cops or what?" His face had now settled down to a malleable landscape. His eyebrows were lifted. He gripped the table softly and leaned towards me.

"No, I don't think so, Nat. Not sure," I replied. "I'm pulled in two directions. The cops gave it up as a weather-related mishap. Why did they do that? Was it a cover up? Who was behind it? But this was a small plane. Not a big target like the Air India plane and the tapes that got erased." My throat dried as I tried to explain. "I want to kind of sleuth around on my own, you know, when I'm not busy. See what I can find out. But I also want to know the girl better."

"I'm with you, man. Lemme look around. Maybe I can find her." A smile then spread on his face. We left it like that. I felt good I knew him so well. And that he cared. Knowing him was like having an accomplice without an agenda. Someone who understood with his eyes and took decisive action without being noticed, without being told.

In the weeks that followed, I maintained my routine of working four full days at the courier company, racking up a total of thirty-two hours per week, and then spending a day hanging about in the cafés, taking notes. Broken china pieces moved in slow motion through the air around me, turning, twisting, taunting, almost fitting and then separating to float again before looking for a different mating piece. There was a design to all of it and I would fit them together: a mesmerizing snowfall on a painting on a wall, a receptionist smacking her gums with disdain, a lady in shades with a Mercedes in an arrogant hurry, a chiropractor flying to the Caribbean without notice, waybills with invented names, explosions in mid-air, and a cold case shut mercilessly.

In the evenings, I walked around the neighbourhood, trying to avoid Boulevard St-Laurent. I'd walk through the back alleys where Chinese, Vietnamese, Greek, Polish, Algerian, and Québécois cooks, bakers, orange peelers and onion choppers, sous-chefs and cleaver-wielders took cigarette breaks sitting on the steps, where cyclists whizzed by recklessly, where gloves, needles, emptied prophylactic foils and silly stuff like that all rolled about together near dumpsters, and spray can artists smiled at you before they bombed nondescript brick walls with bulbous alphabet bottoms that looked like they were humping each other in a continuous procession. I continued through corner parks, past *dépanneurs* where orange-haired Thai waiters stood with muscular shoulders, looked up at the balconies to see chubby Portuguese women with stumpy elbows leaning against wrought-iron rails, always seemingly disgusted by the goings-on down below.

Every such encounter was good for my soul, forcing me to rethink coordinates, helping me slow the constant swirl of broken china.

Sometimes a door flung open and I'd see a busboy rush out to expertly throw several garbage bags into an open dumpster before rushing away again. In the unexpected light, I'd see at the edge of the parking lot a couple against a doorway, skirt lifted above the hips and pants folding around the knees.

CHAPTER FIVE

The Way It Happened
at the Majestic

It happened as arranged.

"Bed and breakfast, you come and you go, you pay and you stay, no make trouble, no make nonsense."

Mrs. Karamanlis runs the small hotel between Avenue Coloniale and St-Laurent, one block north of Avenue du Mont-Royal. It has twenty rooms on three floors, some with attached bathrooms, though most without, and is more like an *auberge* than a hotel, which doesn't stop it from being called The Hôtel Majestic. Perhaps Mrs. Karamanlis thinks the lobby is majestic. It is certainly elaborate. The furniture at the front—for the space is large—has an art deco influence, and yet as one makes one's way toward the back, the furniture, if one is in a generous mood, can be considered Victorian. There the sunlight streams in at a sharp angle from small, high windows in two recessed alcoves.

Recently, an Italian friend from the neighbourhood sent me a link to a video of a hotel in Venice in which he stayed. I think the Hôtel Majestic has an identical sense of fading incoherence.

Mrs. Karamanlis sits at the far end of the lobby, staring into the doorway like a jail warden. Usually there is no place to eat and no food is served, but in the morning—briefly—appears a breakfast table with croissants, Danish pastries, muffins, two pots of coffee, one decaffeinated, and a pot of tea. Everyone pays for breakfast. There's a helper of Portuguese origin who looks like Susan Boyle before the makeover. She appears and disappears from behind the curtain grunting and sweating. Every day she serves breakfast, tidies the rooms, changes the linen, and cleans the washrooms. A young man comes by every second day to vacuum the corridors and the lobby. I know, because I review her general ledger on a regular basis.

She has a perfectly legal liquor licence, unfortunately expired; she claims she does not sell liquor. All the bottles are kept under the counter. You don't know what whisky you'll get until she's pouring. Do not ask for single malt. You will get "jez whishhky," meaning the blended stuff from Seagram's or a Johnny Walker Red, or maybe even inexpensive Bourbon: it all qualifies. She has a small fridge where she keeps ice cubes.

Whisky? "Yesh."

Vodka? "Yesh."

Rum? "No! No mixers. Only straight. No martini. No beer."

Cognac and brandy? "Maybe…"

Ouzo? "Oh! Yeah!"

You might get some peanuts, pretzels, or Lay's chips on the side. It all depends on her sense of ritual at the moment. If she knows you well she might open a bag of small pitas and place them on a plate with a dollop of *taramosalata* or *tzatziki*.

There isn't a computer at the front desk, only the large ledger. The first entry is from before 1970. There is a carefully guarded board behind her where she hangs all the keys. Most of the clients who reserve rooms have heard about the place from other business types, or maybe the Automobile Agency. Unsavoury elements are discouraged by aggressive questioning and advance deposits. If you come in with a backpack she gives you a thorough once-over. The rooms are well preserved and clean. The floors creak, but the linen is fresh and there are no bugs. Water pressure is decent.

As she has made clear to me several times, she discourages one-nighters. "I donna want no shady people; mekke this my hotel like a den, like, you know? No mekke the shady here." It's her reputation she's concerned about: once marked in this neighbourhood one is marked for life, although I don't know how she thinks she can control it. I'm pretty sure "shly" folks do violate her standards, despite the power and threat of her menacing Mediterranean eyebrows.

I call myself Chuck Bhatt, she calls me "Hey! Chudd". I have corrected her a few times but she persists, so I don't bother anymore. She goes every now and then to the *dépanneur* at the corner of Prince Arthur to buy biscuits. She likes Oreos. I was helping the owner there with his accounts when she asked me "Hey Chudd, come by shometime and look at my booksh." That's how I got to know her.

I'm not an accountant, but I'm good at keeping a general ledger and bringing forward the accounts from one page to the next. I do it for the courier company on an accounting package and understand the logic. Of course, she doesn't think of computerizing herself. "Whash that?" she says, her eyebrows raised as if I had proposed contracting a skin disease. There are times I bring along my laptop, run a small accounting package, and re-categorize the entries. Then I print it out and give it to her. She dutifully pastes it on a fresh page in the same large ledger book in preparation for her tax accountant and auditor. In return, she says I can use the lobby to meet friends. In fact, she occasionally serves us coffee and cookies, and even once fried calamari. I consider myself a privileged acquaintance.

Now, here is where a strange thing happened. Like, I am on to this plane crash thing, my sense of guilt had ravaged me beyond any notion of salvation and am also trying to find this gum-chewing girl. For a while I had been getting a series of strange emails. Normally they'd automatically go into the spam box, but these, for whatever reason, outmanoeuvred the filters and managed to reach me.

"We've met a few times. We have a common friend. You may know me but maybe you don't."

I guessed it was a woman, although she didn't disclose much about herself. She was interested in meeting me, writing, *"Maybe you would be interested in stuff I know."* That teaser sounded tacky, but I was attracted to the straight-forwardness of her approach.

I had almost convinced myself it was Myra, but then I realized I was simply believing what I wanted to believe. Myra wouldn't write that way. The emails had a different personality. Besides, despite my long and faithful vigils, Myra hadn't appeared at any of the various cafés and pubs she used to visit. She had clearly abandoned me, leaving me alone to research the mid-air explosion over Trois-Pistoles, an avoidable tragedy in which I was painfully complicit.

Then the woman sending the emails informed me she was taking tango lessons on Thursday evenings. At that moment, I was hooked.

Now tango is by far the most suggestive, stimulating, heat-transferring, pheromone-flying dance form conceivable. It is not sullen like most European dances. It is pure scarlet with a dash of black: it takes one to the edge and then dangerously hesitates before pulling one back. There are other art forms committed to rapture, but I think tango is in a tantric-hot class by itself.

Not that I have any real experience with it.

I remember Carlos Saura's film. I went to see it with a relative, then visiting Montreal, and it sent exhilarating and unexpected chills up and down my spine. It hadn't been hard for the only attractive cousin I have to cajole me into taking evening courses with her on the second floor of a very masculine building on St-Viateur. It was there that I learned many women—maybe most—dance as a way of exploring their own bodies. A lot of the male students didn't know that when a woman invited them to dance it wasn't with amorous intentions, but as a necessary launch-pad to better explore their own physical being. My cousin bluntly confirmed my tentative insight into the excitement of the male students, many in leather pants, who raced up the stairs to the weekly practice, "Yeah, well, men are like that. Dopes. Our bodies, ourselves, get it?"

In any case the film, set in Buenos Aires, is the story of a director who finds himself bent upon making the ultimate tango movie. While doing so he falls in love with the girlfriend of the tough guy who is funding the film. Now if you are like me and don't want to end up rotting in a dumpster on the outskirts of Buenos Aires, you'd find a way to avoid such an obviously precarious sequence of events. Nevertheless, the film was an extraordinary accomplishment, and remembering it again I knew I wasn't about to walk away from the person who sent the email. Not as long as I had scarlet liquids simmering through my veins.

When I told Mrs. Karamanlis of my plan to meet this new friend in a room in her hotel her eyebrows arched to such great heights that I knew I had erred.

"You Chudd, you shurprishe me! You, I thinksh was not like them!" Her eyebrows went through several wave-like inflections which I couldn't help considering as aftershocks.

I explained that I had suggested her premises only because I'd be meeting a friend who was bringing along music to show me tango steps, and that I didn't know where else I might find both sufficient space and suitable privacy. I very magically made a virtue out of the fact that I wasn't inviting this woman to my own tiny loft. But to her grand unstained, reputable *chambre.*

"Right, Chudd!" she said, with more delegitimizing, wriggling eyebrows, which slowly subsided. Then she smiled decisively, "Okay! I trusht my book-keeper."

I had the place, which was what mattered, and I could live with one night of utter shame as a book-keeper with out-of-control lust. I entered the suite to look around and get a feel for it. The furniture in the adjoining room had a rich burgundy finish. There were old pictures in sepia tones hanging tastefully along the walls beneath ornate ceiling work. There were doors that had brass plates, marble pedestals with brass flower vases, a red carpet in good condition and two yellowing chandeliers that had all the bulbs intact. There was an old-style mirror with dark veins running through it above a fake fireplace. In another corner, Victorian-style furniture was placed around a polished granite coffee table. The legs of all the chairs were curved and expressive, as if comfortable and well rested. There was a desk in the corner that had three drawers on either side and, on top, two slide-out drawers with a carefully carved arch over the centre. A lit lamp was on it.

I sent off an email with the date, time, and place. She agreed to meet.

On the awaited evening, Mrs. Karamanlis opened the door to my room and turned around, hands on her hips in what can only be considered an admonishing manner, but with a cooperative conspiracy in her gaze. I smiled and thanked her, then held out my hand. She gave me the keys and smiled in return.

"You are cute, you!" she said.

I had brought a small vase with two roses, two bottles of Australian Shiraz, a small tablecloth with lace at the edges which my mother had given me years ago, two wine glasses, and Belgian pastries from a shop on Avenue du Parc. I laid out the tablecloth carefully on the bedside table and put the corkscrew next to the wine bottles, at an angle. Mrs. Karamanlis had thought fit to give me two plates and two dessert forks, which she came by and left for me. I had put on a black corduroy jacket over a dark sweater and wore a pair of Kenneth Cole shoes bought at 50 percent off at Winners. I ensured that the shine on them was immaculate. I was excited, but also mystified: whoever Malia was—for she had finally shared her name—I would meet her at 7 p.m. I turned on the TV, kept the volume low and pretended to watch.

By 7:30 p.m. she still had not come. I was impatient, although there was nothing I could do, not having her cellphone number. At about 7:45 p.m. I started pacing the floor and running my fingers through my hair. I heard a radio playing softly in the distance, but couldn't tell where it was coming from. I tried hard to listen, but in the constant din of street noises and passing cars I couldn't hear the beat. At a certain point, the music rose in volume and I realized it was definitely a tango, like a brassy version of *La Cumparsita*. It rose and fell. My insides leapt and collapsed. I was not ready for such games.

I waited another hour, frankly irate, the music still playing, and by 9 p.m. I was imagining all sorts of possibilities. I thought I heard brisk movements on the floor above me in tune with the music, but I couldn't be sure. At 9:15 p.m. I stepped out of the room and carefully looked up and down the corridor. Not a soul anywhere. Listening attentively, I realized that the tango was coming from the floor above. Meanwhile, I heard the distinctive sounds of erotic activity from the room opposite. I was infuriated by the heaving and breathing that was discovering its own quickening rhythm. I was now certain I was hearing things that weren't actually there. Perhaps I had even made up the lady in the Mercedes-Benz. Nothing was real, except for my conviction of having been duped.

I needed to do something. After walking back and forth, I returned to my room and opened the bottle of wine and started to drink. It seemed Malia was not going to show up. I reasoned that she had played a game and the tango from afar was a cruel joke. Around 10 p.m. I was well into the second bottle. After waiting for nearly three hours, I rose unsteadily and noticed that the tablecloth was stained by my careless pouring. At just that moment I heard the loud sound of a mirror or a window being smashed. The tango stopped.

I stepped out of my room and the man across the hallway had also opened his door. He was wearing a towel around his waist and I could see behind him a woman sitting on the bed with the covers barely above her breasts. She looked satisfied. I didn't say anything. He retreated after shrugging his shoulders.

I finished off the second bottle of wine, packed up the tablecloth and the vase, threw the roses out, put the two glasses in my briefcase, and descended to the lobby. Mrs. Karamanlis was not there. Her nephew Dino was behind the desk. I gave him the key and paid my bill. I looked around. Was it true what the chairs in the lobby, facing each other, were saying to each other? Loser? Really? Was anything true? It was then that it struck me. I asked Dino if a certain lady had asked for me.

"Yes, of course! I sent her to Room 310 with the spare keys." He said this with easy confidence and a suggestive smile.

"But I was in Room 210! Didn't you tell her?" I was beginning to see floaters shaped like stars and knives in the corners of my eyes.

"No! The boss said you were in 310. Everything cool?" He pushed forward a handwritten note from Mrs. Karamanlis that said '#310, lady for Chudd'. "She was pretty mad, you know, when she left! She stormed out with her radio and threw the key on the counter. I figured something must have happened. Is everything okay, Chuck?"

This fucking insanely laid-back kid with no concept of the nature of my evening was asking if I was okay! Although, to be fair, at least he had my name right.

I abandoned the Hôtel Majestic in an intoxicated, melancholic, state; the kind of night where the moon is an unwanted follow spot and inebriated crowds spill out from the clubs wanting to fight. My body bounced from lamppost to lamppost, hitting every youth to mid-life chicane possible in a two hundred-metre walk home. I landed on my bed around midnight.

It was 1 p.m. the next day when I finally arose to call my boss and say that I couldn't make the afternoon shift. She didn't sound happy.

I checked my emails. It was brutal.

"You thought you could dick me around, didn't you? You thought I'd just turn up like I did and it didn't matter that you were holed up with another chick? I even brought my blaster so we could tango and what did you do? Stuck

it to me! So, you can shove it! And by the way, you pay for the smashed-up mirror! Okay? Because they don't have my whereabouts and you're not getting them, either. It was your idea to meet there and you pay for it. Know what I mean? If it wasn't for that friend of yours, I wouldn't have bothered. He told me you were a sincere Indian dude with some Armenian mix or something. He egged me on. Sincere, my ass! What is it with you fucking guys who hang around the Plateau? Don't you have any backbone? And let me tell you as well, I was not all wet thinking of you, there were things I wanted to discuss. Don't bother. —Malia"

I was totally at a loss as to how this could have happened. Had Mrs. Karamanlis done it deliberately, or had it been an honest mistake? I went back two nights later to confront her. She appeared angry but not livid. Nor did she try to extract any compensation from me for the broken mirror. "Chudd! I told you I don't like theesh types! They break the mirror; they make the messh and leave!" She said that from a distance, drying the glasses behind the bar, not looking me in the eye.

I was fearless, knowing I had done nothing wrong. "I'm sorry about what happened, but why did you send her to the floor above? She and I waited for three hours, each in the wrong room. She thinks I stood her up."

Mrs. Karamanlis rolled her eyes. "Yes, I shcrewed up and Dino shoulda been smarter, but he wasn't. He's a shtupido, you know. Sho we're even. Sho I forget the broken mirror. You want to meet her again?" She looked at me with eyebrows lifting and a sparkle gathering. I knew then that she wanted me to continue with the ledgering.

But it was her handwriting. Why had she done it?

CHAPTER SIX

Like a Warm Blanket

"Dear Malia, you will probably not believe me but I was in the room below all along and heard you play the tango and then break the mirror. I didn't know it was you. I sat there waiting and after you still hadn't come three hours later, I finished off the two bottles of wine I had wanted to share and went home feeling hopeless, not knowing you were mad as hell right above me and rightfully so. The lady who owns the hotel either played a mean trick on me by sending you to the wrong room or she made a genuine error. I apologize for the screw-up, but I still want to meet you. I would like to know you better. I will be at the Café Palmas on Friday evening at 7 p.m. if you wish to meet me. Awaiting hopefully, Chuck."

She never turned up.

Given the evidence of Nat's role in setting up an encounter that wasn't, I figured I should share the bad news with him. I flagged him down as he cycled along Boulevard St-Joseph. Recently back from auditioning in New York, he wore a sleeveless cycling jersey which showed his muscles, taut and glistening. He shared a brilliant smile.

"So, how's it goin'?" he asked.

I assured him it had been a disaster, and that if he'd been the one who arranged it he should've told me, instead of putting me through such a complicated arrangement. I explained all that had happened and he was genuinely amused, as I thought he would be.

"So, who was it?" I asked.

His smile turned mischievous. He wouldn't divulge, which is why I suddenly knew. "Myra?"

"Of course!" he said, with a wry look. "But I didn't tell her it was the guy she'd met at the chiropractor's office. I wanted her to be surprised. I told her you were a friend, an interesting dude, and it would be good if the two of you met. You can't beat up on me, bro!"

As usual, he was charming and I was disarmed. "I do want to meet her. It was good being in email contact with her, even if she was Malia at the time. She was attractive and straightforward. I liked that. Now it's all fucked up."

Not only was Nat surprised by the turn of events, he thought it offered a curious twist to the explosion over Trois-Pistoles and how I'd learned about it. "It all adds to the narrative, doesn't it? Look! It's an amazing story that continues to grow! You gotta follow up, man! This isn't goin' away. You said you wanted to write." He pointed to my head. "You got a story brewing there, no? Up there! Pot-a-gold, man!"

It worried me that Myra of the chance encounter was so different from Malia of the emails. Although the last email had been in character. I could see the pout on Myra's mouth as she fired it off.

We continued to Café Palmas and each of us ordered a pint. Nat was cheerful and confident, strange given that he casually mentioned he hadn't been successful at any of the recent auditions, either in New York or Toronto. He told me he wanted lead roles, not the marginal characters in sci-fi shoots being offered around Montreal. He had limits, he said, principles. At that point he lowered his head, stared into his glass, and told me he was considering his options.

"What options?" I was blunt.

"Damn! So, she was actually there all that time?" He was avoiding my question. "And the bitch Karamanlis pretended she didn't know? Like a Coen brothers' script, man! All you need is a sociopathic killer, a fake kidnapping, and then someone tossed from a fire escape! Surreal! Great!" He had no intention of answering me.

"My ass! Not so surreal for me!" I said in a sulk. "I even brought along two glasses and a pair of roses to go with the two bottles. I had to drink both of them myself. It didn't help I was hung over the whole next day."

He laughed and then, suddenly serious, stared frankly into my eyes and asked if I was going to write her.

"You think I need a woman that bad? Are you pimping for me?"

I lied. A lie for the self, a lie for the listener, and yet another, freely given away to anyone who wants to believe what is clearly not true.

Nat knew. His heart was like a soccer field in spring, open and clean. I couldn't hide from him. "Okay, okay," I relented, "I already wrote her and she didn't respond. But I don't want you setting things right." I tried not to show my irritation. "I need to do it myself."

"I'm with you all the way. You figure it out, man! I got other things to do." His cool was electric. A charged cool, which I liked. She was insane. Possibly dangerous.

We chatted for another hour and parted at ten. I went back to my apartment while he headed off on his bike to his mother's. I watched him getting smaller. He was clearly happier and in good physical shape. But he hadn't shared his *options*.

He'd been in all the school plays. In our senior year, he directed the annual production while I ran the light board. We were coaxial in some ways, rotating around with the same opinions: everyone knew if he didn't like something I wouldn't either, and vice versa. "Thick like *dakoos*," my grandpa would say. Like dacoits, brigands, thieves . . . he meant it in a loving way. One looked after the other. Nat had always called me when he felt like doing something. If we didn't do something together it was because one of us was out of town. If I didn't hear from him there was something wrong. It was inconceivable to me, and I suspect to him as well, that we would consciously deceive each other. "I'm gonna go to New York and be in the movies! Nothing's gonna stop me!" He had laughed as he said that during our final year in high school.

No one in Nat's family had gone to college. His grandparents on his father's side had emigrated from Russia to New York in the early 1900s and later moved to Montreal. They were not particularly religious, although they had made monuments even in the old country. Nat's father was like a gnome. He rarely spoke. He moved through his tombstone maze like a child, hopping in and out, running his hands over the granite and marble, calling in his workmen to highlight flaws. He worked furiously, his sallow muscular arms dripping with sweat. I'd stand outside the fence as Nat tried to catch his attention. He'd appear suddenly from behind a large tombstone and nod quietly. Then he'd be gone.

His wife, on the other hand, Mrs. Meeropol, yearned for an opportunity to talk. She'd stop and chat whenever we met at the newly renovated grocery store on St-Laurent. She was tall, ineffably handsome, and walked like a film star from the fifties, gracefully. Her hair was bobbed and fell about her shoulders. She wore long skirts, sunglasses, and fire-red lipstick. It made for an extremely vivacious smile. Her husband was rarely seen with her. "Hello Chuck! Come by sometime and join me for tea." Electric invitation.

And I'd nod my head. "Yes, Mrs. Meeropol. I will. Soon! I don't need Nat's permission, I know!"

She was fond of me. Every time I went over she sat me down, elegant and exquisite, and we chatted. She had the air of a celebrity, a quality that clung to her naturally, as if she were forever the calm, in a sea of tumultuous admirers. She always found interesting incidents to discuss. That was her forte, remembering unusual things from the past that no one else thought to bring up.

The front door to their house had two entrances, like a duplex. Theirs was the one on the left. It was a neat, small green door with a window frame on top. You took your boots off and left them outside on the black mat. The narrow stairs, polished Canadian oak, rose straight up. They were slippery. You had to be careful in winter when wearing thick socks. Hidden helium lights on the ceiling lit the way. The vivid colours from numerous paintings and photographs jumped out from the walls. There was no depressing darkness anywhere, no web of cracks in the plaster, no creaking stairs. The wood hadn't been darkened by veneer.

The landing above the stairs had a wall with a built-in bookshelf. There must have been several hundred books in it. I knew Nat's father was not a reader, so it was Mrs. Meeropol who collected them, discovering vast new territories across mountains and rivers from her Bagg Street home. There were mostly history books interspersed with a selection of novels, both known and unknown. There was also a stereo system on it. Faintly audible melismatic chants seeped from the bookshelf speakers. I asked if she listened to Buddhist music and she laughed and answered, "No, no, neutral. I find it soothing."

She liked the songs that drew from different ethnicities and left me with the impression of nomads wandering in a high steppe among plunging mountains and valleys before one prodded the sheep home at dusk.

She had a small corner in which the books she currently read lay strewn, page-marked, on a glass-topped coffee table. Behind that was a large lamp that curved over the reading area and spread circular warmth onto the shaggy rug beneath the leather chaise longue. There was in her face the longing to share ideas, and I knew that Nat was impervious to that. It's strange, but parents create resentment in their children to their own passionate interests. Nat wouldn't give her the time of day.

Whenever I visited, she sat me down, served tea with biscuits, and explored the possibilities of some new topic. She might begin by asking about my work or something simple like that, and then refer my answer to a recent book she'd acquired. Sometimes I felt honoured—and sometimes I just felt sad.

If the conversation went well she sometimes expressed pleasure with herself. "My friends say I'm an elitist but I dismiss that totally. I look at things fresh. Without the tint. Neutral!" This she said with a gentle, mischievous smile. And she told me stories about the Main I can't forget. The spirits gathered as the fog hung low.

"Oh! Yes, they are all slowly fading away. You get to talk to so many people. Is it not?"

"People came here to work, sell, and grow families. They lived above the stores. Some sold stuff they made or grew themselves. There were crisp pickles in big wooden vats in the windows. You see the street lamps? They don't have the same glow they used to have. It was different before. You walked down the street and there would be a haze hanging over like a low cloud, you know, like protection. People walked slowly and hung around outside their stores. Everyone knew each other. When new immigrants came, we all helped out and took them in. The women—they wore long skirts even when pushing carts around—would band together to help the new arrivals. Yeah?"

I had no reason to disagree with her. "How long ago was this?" I asked, taking mental notes for my diary, as I saw black and white images building up in my mind.

"Oh! Not too long ago. Moshe was still in Brooklyn. His dad was running the business here. Everyone thought Moshe was too short to join, you know, just five feet five inches! Then he brought Moshe here in the early fifties and my mother moved from New York after the war. We both spoke Yiddish. His family was strictly Russian. Mine was a mix of Russian, Polish, and maybe some German. We got married here in that synagogue across the street. There was a printing press right there on the other side and across was the big Warshaw's market with the deli close by. I was twenty and he was twenty-five when we got married. All the Catholics went to the school on the corner of Clark and Bagg. It was called Devonshire. Jews couldn't attend Catholic schools, so most went to Protestant schools instead. Ha!"

I figured she must be in her late seventies, but she looked like she was in her late fifties. She must have had Nat pretty late in her life. The skin on her face was still flawless, like a polished apple, smooth, pink, with a blush of red.

"Most of the buildings you see now were built in the 1890s. Dogs were allowed to roam everywhere. Some had leashes, but most didn't. They peed in little squirts all over the place and sauntered across the street like they owned it! Most of the big houses were owned by the Weinstein family. Lot of cold water flats. They owned all sorts of businesses, importing stuff from Russia, Poland, and Hungary. Sometimes they made stuff here for export: furniture, food, pickles, sausages, cheese. They also ran the housing business, you know, and quite a few were lawyers. They lived here, traded here, and died here. There was no other place to go. The synagogues were all here, too." Then she sighed.

"When Moshe got involved in the business, his father told him it wasn't just a business but a service to the community. Look up at the sky, he said, and you'll see, if you're doing well, there'll be a fog above that looks down at you. The Chinese came and settled further south, where Chinatown is now. There was a fog over Chinatown too, near de La Gauchetière. That's where all the bars were during prohibition. The Americans came to drink and dance with the girls. Imagine, no girly bars in New York! So they came here. I went to one of the dance bars with Moshe. You know he was short, so we moved around with me leading most of the time. His knees reached my shin, barely. Most of the time he'd sit down and I'd dance with others. Yeah?" She said all that with a big smile on her face, breathless.

I listened to her with absolute adulation. "Tell me more about the fog. I don't see a fog here anymore."

"I don't know, I don't know. It was more like a dome than a pall." She stopped and looked out through the back window, distracted. Then she began again, more concentrated this time. "You know, I guess the streets weren't as warm as they are now. We had nearly four whole months of good warm summer weather. And six months or so of clean hard winter. None of this back and forth, one day warm, next day freezing like now. The heat in the cold months didn't rise as high. The lights didn't give out so much heat either, and they were lower. So, there was fog hanging low around each lamp; a nice, diffused glow like in a Van Gogh—you know? There were real neighbourhoods then, Jewish, Portuguese, some Greeks, then Little Italy further north. In the Jewish stretch, all the way up to Rachel, there were Hungarians, Russians, Slovaks, Poles, Austrians, and Bavarians. The snow was powdery on the ground and the tramcars went by noiselessly. The snow remained white in the winter. It didn't get caked with mud. I guess there weren't that many cars. The night was quiet and friendly. Not noisy. My mother came here with me when I was ten years old. She had lost her husband in the war. He was a partisan in Yugoslavia who went into the mountains and never came back. So, my mother moved to Montreal with me because she heard there was a needle trade business here. Her family encouraged her. We had an uncle who came with us, and he arranged for us to stay at a friend's house further north near Parc. But my mom didn't like it there. She wanted to live on St-Laurent, so we rented a flat from the Weinsteins and lived in a building near Rue Rachel. That's when I met Moshe. He came out of the fog walking toward me! You know what I mean! Like from nowhere! I was only a teenager. We had met once in Brooklyn and recognized each other. There was a bakery at the street corner and for three cents we got Langos, like a Hungarian flatbread with some cheese in it. Then we walked up and down the street. His pants were falling down because his hips were not so wide and his hat flew off in a gust of wind and we laughed. You still want to know what the fog was all about?"

"Yes, Mrs. Meeropol, I want to know."

"It was like a tenderness of the soul transferred from one generation to the next. A yearning for the villages we had left behind, for the factories and ghettoes that were ghost towns now, a quest for quietness when all the guns kept on pounding.

"It was like an inaudible grief that came with the refugee mindset of being displaced. People didn't talk much about it. They simply nodded their heads and observed the rituals.

"The fog was like a cover; a warm blanket through which you could see the stars if you wanted. There was not so much parody on the streets, no relentless mockery. There were large writings and advertisements on the brick walls, awnings freshly painted to match the shops next door. There was, how do you say, conviviality? There was art, too; paintings in the shops, always. Beautiful paintings everywhere. Even if it was a sausage seller! And in the night, the lamps glowed within the fog hanging low over everyone. People looked out of their second-floor windows and called out gently to their neighbours. The fog wasn't a fog. It was a feeling." She laughed out loud, startled by her own words.

CHAPTER SEVEN

Pieces of Napkin

Have you seen Myra lately? Have you seen the girl who walks around aimlessly? I sat making notes with my back to the big glass windows in Merise's Bar. My sign off on a waybill had helped destroy a civilian airplane gliding innocently above a pristine green riverine landscape; I had been the final cog in a murder plot that had obliterated the dreams of others.

The west side of the bar was lit with bright sunlight prowling in at an exploratory angle. Then the light bounced off the white, un-tanned shoulders of a young woman who had a sea-horse tattooed on her muscular arms before spilling onto the burgundy stained sides of the bar and counter. I knew her skin must have been burning. I could sense it, as she rubbed her shoulders gently with the palm of her hands. I stared at her arm, thinking of Myra.

Nat careened by on his bike. I wanted to run out and call to him, but he was pedalling too fast. He wouldn't have noticed me. Outside the window, pink geraniums wobbled amusingly, prodded by an erratic summer breeze. The un-tanned woman remained where she was, firmly gripping her Griffon Blonde, staring at her tabloid with barely open eyes. The rays of the bona fide summer sun, available scarcely four months a year, continued to highlight her shoulders.

I had seen this girl cycling around the Plateau. She looked athletic. I think she was a personal trainer at the Y on Parc Ave, and during the day worked as a translator. Yes, Nat had said that about her.

It occurred to me that people knew each other in this part of town in a special kind of way. If you needed a recording engineer, common names would crop up from several sources. If you were looking for a video editor, a cameraman, a story editor, a carpenter, or a translator, you could ask the barman and have several names in no time. If you talked to a musician you could get the contacts for someone who had a private studio in the Townships, and then your best friend would corroborate and give you the same phone number. If you wanted a notary, there were many, but everyone knew all of them and had an opinion on each. If you needed an Egyptologist, she was actually the pianist in the combo two doors over in the next bar. One lounge singer's bass player is his cousin's lover, and probably good at fixing brakes. People seemed to know about each other like worms in a dark soil, like a row of nervous peas snug in a pod. It was a world where one skill was never enough. It seemed to follow that everyone was observant, competitive, and incestuous but living precariously from one temporary job to another.

I stared at the nicely tattooed arms of the woman. I looked outside, and in the distance, someone was striding across St-Laurent in a long skirt. I stood up and narrowed my eyes. I sat back down. Not her.

Somewhere else not too far away, the woman with the dark shades was getting into her Benz.

I picked up the weekly tabloid and started leafing through the classifieds in the back. Amongst the escort service ads, the bankruptcy sales, and the second-hand laptop giveaways was a quarter-page ad announcing "*Careers abroad for men and women in good physical shape, of strong mental character, keen for adventure. Learn new skills in the surveillance and protection industry."*

The personal trainer with the sea-horse tattoo got up, paid at the bar, and left. I watched her walking towards the Main, every step a controlled display of muscular awareness. She could apply for that job in the "protection industry." She began to turn the corner where there's a slight curve in the road, and I leaned back in my chair to look at her one more time.

The May sun was finally streaming in, as it should, and my back felt comfortably warm. There was still a Montreal chill in the air outside, where the sun missed the sidewalk; a nip that made you wish you had left home wearing a base-ball cap and had high collars and large side pockets in your sweatshirt. I was wearing a sweater and cobbling away at a vegetarian chili that the Portuguese waitress had served. I had known her a while. She was friendly and carefree. Once Nat and I had been sitting at the bar on a busy night and the shoulder strap of her blouse kept sliding off, revealing an attractive upper arm and the hint of an equally energetic upper torso. She didn't seem to care, smiled at both of us and filled our glasses. At some point, while she was carrying a full tray of beer mugs, Nat lifted her strap and put it over her shoulder. She'd appreciated that. Was he "keen for adventure abroad?" What were the options he was considering?

Now alone, she listened distractedly to a large man. I say large because the floors in Merise's don't usually creak when someone walks. With this guy, the floor audibly suffered as he shifted his chassis from side to side, moving his weight from foot to foot, snorting heavily through his pock-marked nose. If he would just sit down, it'd be fine. Maybe the bar stool was too petite for his XXXL arse. I decided I had endured this long enough and laid my shades on the counter in a firm gesture with a distinct click, then supplemented that with a direct and hostile stare. It didn't register.

The students at the back, however, where the tabletops have chess and scrabble boards laminated on top, were trying to concentrate. Despite their habitual use of the requisite iPod earphones, the creaking overwhelmed them, too, and they acted disturbed. The waitress looked at the large man with antipathy. He was not only brash and noisy, he insisted on flirting with her in broken French, idiomatic Portuguese, and dismantled English. She, on the other hand, was perfectly bilingual and also spoke a bit of rough Portuguese. Whenever he looked away, she looked at me sideways and rolled her eyes. At some point she hastened over to ask if the chili was good. Then she returned with more nachos and sour cream, but I wasn't in the mood to redeem her from her compatriot. In fact, I enjoyed her discomfort. I knew the man, had seen him around, a heavy-breathing know-it-all who had a part-time job at the fish store at the corner of Avenue des Pins. I used to see him against the back door of the store wearing a bloodied apron and holding a large curved fish knife. There were fish scales, octopus parts, gills, and entrails sticking to his apron. He was usually panting heavily then, too.

Trying to avoid him, she kept retreating to the far side of the bar to adjust the draft beer handles, clean out some pans, make a fresh pot of coffee, and attempt to ignore his overtures. The man snorted and smiled, trying to entice her back to his side.

Finally, I decided to save her. I still hadn't seen Myra, so I asked, "Have you seen Myra Banks lately? You know, the girl who does bit roles in TV ads and movies." I didn't have to say more. She came as near to me as the bar would allow and, shaking her chest left to right and back, pouting a lip sliding smile, asked "You mean this one?"

The Portuguese big guy couldn't help but notice her little breast-bouncing impression and looked at me with curiosity.

"Yeah, well...*maybe* that one." I answered sadly. Having met Myra the few occasions I had, I wasn't convinced she deserved the reputation.

"Yeah, yeah! She's been coming around. Sometimes she's alone with her large shades on, sometimes she's with a different guy . . . you know what I mean." Her response felt like a pair of sharp crab pincers closing in at the core of my heart.

"She was here a few days ago with the guy who roller-blades everywhere, you know, the Meeropol kid? They're both actors." She said this with so much disdain for Myra that I felt she was herself in love with Nat and wanted Myra out of the way. "He's a serious guy: got career goals, a family business, you know? But, like, her, I don't know, what does she do? She told me she was working at an office and then got fired. So now she walks around in a way that's not too cool, you know? She got this tattoo on her arm which isn't all that bad actually, as far as that kind of tattoo goes. She hangs around. Too demonstrative, you know?"

I hadn't seen a tattoo on Myra. "She's not a walker," I said firmly. "I know that. Just going through a bad patch."

The pudgy Portuguese fishmonger finally realized he had completely lost the woman's attention and chose to shuffle out, braying adieus loudly and blowing a kiss. It was truly sad.

I had torn up the napkin in front of me. I had written a thought on each of the small pieces: fog, diamonds, Myra, Malia, infidelity, insurance, plane, Mercedes, tango, Johnny Depp, Mrs. Meeropol, diaspora, empire, painting, Nat, migrants, river. Then I had pushed them all into a small pile. The bartender considered this with a curious expression, smiled, then returned to the middle of her now-quiet bar.

I recognized that Myra might not be totally well adjusted. Her mum was stand-offish, distant, and determinedly conceited. She, on the other hand, was lively, feisty, and friendly. Apparently, she had told Nat, "I gotta find something totally groovy, something occupying! I need to immerse myself in it. I hate these short stints doing stuff here and there. I want a long, torrid affair . . . with cinema! Whaddya say? I want it to happen, Nat."

For me, the logic of that quote clarified her character. Somehow, as confused and diffused as it was, it made perfect sense. Nat had also told me that she was bored easily, pointing to the smacking sounds she made while chewing gum as empirical evidence.

Okay, I could accept that.

"You're still interested in her, huh?" he had said with a weird smile. I lied in return, "Maybe, maybe. But maybe not! I'm not sure."

Hell, I was attracted to her like crazy!

Her mother had a French last name but moved in the Anglo milieu. There must be a story behind that. According to Nat, Myra had acted in quite a few English plays but periodically dropped out of sight. No one knew where she had gone or what she was doing. The unpredictability had eventually cost her her reputation. I understood, but I didn't agree.

So my overwhelming attraction to Myra was compounded by an increasing curiosity and concern for her well-being, though I was loathe to admit it. I tried to rationalize my feelings from a neighbourhood point of view, as if we had to protect each other from constant mislabelling and she was being called a walker. What a pussy I was, making a virtue of intense desire.

Both she and Nat sought personal validation in a world that wouldn't give it. As Nat argued, "It's a tough world, man! Dog-eat-dog! You have it or you don't. The agents are all ma'fuckers! They keep tellin' you—change your parting, get stubble, change your accent—what the fuck am I supposed to do? I don't have a fucking Yiddish accent. I lost it. I don't have an Anglo accent from the 'burbs, either. What do they want? Brooklyn? Huh! I say *doig* already!"

Sometimes I'd see him rollerblading down a side street and then plunge down a wheelchair access to careen onto the pavement at an impossible angle before coming to a dead halt. He had that manoeuvre down, but it wasn't satisfying. Since his dad had passed on, he'd been looking for ways to get more auditions in New York, without luck. He worked on his physique; always muscular, he seemed to be getting stronger and stronger. Security business, said the ad.

Malia didn't reply to my email. Although I now knew that Nat had set up our meeting, I still waited for an email from her without his involvement. The failed tryst at the Majestic had almost done me in. I was attracted to her and wanted to meet, but on the other hand it wasn't only about her anymore. There was the damned diamond dust. And the plane crash. It was now somewhere between the personal and the moral. The plane crash.

I tried to methodically rearrange the torn shreds of napkin in front of me. But I couldn't find any implicit order, so I finally called Nat. He immediately asked me to come over to Bagg Street. I'd find that a relief, to talk to him and his mom, so I picked up the paper bits and put them in my pocket. Then I said good-bye to the Portuguese waitress whose name had finally come to me: Nathalie.

Nat lived opposite the synagogue. I walked along Roy, passed the back of the fish store, and crossed over onto the shaded side of St-Laurent. I looked up as usual, staring at the facades, the rooftops, the sloping windows, the slate tiles, and the elaborately moulded plaster work along the high edges. I noted again how precarious were the balconies with wrought-iron railings on most of the upper floor apartments. Somewhere, up there, Myra was holed up. But I didn't know where. Nat had never told me and I didn't want to sound too inquisitive, especially after I'd told him to quit pimping for me.

The phone rang: it was Mrs. Meeropol. "Chuck, since you're coming over, would you like to have an early dinner with us?" She liked me. I felt that. I continued briskly.

I'd never had the chance to sit down and chat with Nat's father. He had always been at work, though I'd seen him a few times when I met Nat at the business. His father nodded his head when he saw me, knowing I was from Nat's high school days. He spoke gently and in whispers. I often felt that there was graveness about him. I enjoyed my pun. The fact that his heart had given out and he fell to the pavement and went unnoticed for a long time depressed me. Things like that screw me up. I get overcome. A lot of kids in my generation have a cold, hard attitude about the losses of anyone older. If some kid flipped his lid over drugs, everyone would turn up and hug each other and bring flowers. If there was a hit-and-run everyone turned up wailing and lighting candles. But if someone from an older generation passed on, it was, like . . . normal, even uninteresting. Nat and I were different, perhaps because we had spent so much time with grandparents. We had the patience to sit down and listen while they planted unfinished stories in our heads. And those stories never left me. I'd try to write everything I remembered down whenever I had a spare weekend afternoon, either sitting in my apartment or at one of the bistros on the Main. I kept walking.

We sat down. Mrs. Meeropol brought out some cheese hors d'oeuvres and Nat gulped beer from a bottle while folding clothes in front of the dryer. "What took you so long, man? The lady's been pacin' the floor waitin'." I didn't reply, but I did notice that the ad from the tabloid about the "protection services" was circled with a felt pen and now lay on the coffee table. I went up close to him.

"You're so fucked up. She tells me stuff about the hood that you don't know shit about. It's background material for my epic. Get it? She remembers. You don't. Here! All in here." I took out my notebook in a very officious manner. Stuck my fingers on it. He ignored me, as usual.

"While we have dinner, Chuck, I've thought of a few events that you should know about." She looked at us from the side of her eyes, with a lot of emphasis. Earnestness.

"Oh yeah," he reacted immediately. "Let's begin by trashing the folks who abandoned the hood, then trash the folks who took over the hood, and then trash all those who never came back to the hood. Heh!" She looked at him sharply. They had been arguing.

"They're the ones who owned all the buildings but moved on. They are the smooth operators. They talk from both sides of their mouth. On the one hand they're all high and mighty, even though they're often nasty and crooked. Not exactly the way it's supposed to be, you know! They talk about righteousness like they're the only ones who know what that is, unlike the poorer ones who've lived here all of their lives and loved it and had their kids grow up here and went to the church or the synagogue just over there."

I'd gotten her going. "But that's the way it is with all the communities that have passed through the Main, isn't it?"

"The Portuguese are different. They lived on the upper floor and rented out the lower floors. Some of them bought two houses, adjacent, lived in one and rented the other, but they never bashed others or talked in high and mighty tones. Most of the time they argued about soccer."

I didn't want to contradict her, but several of my friends had Portuguese landlords. When it came to fixing things in the buildings they were ruthless. The moment you asked them to address a leak or a noisy radiator, you could be sure there'd be a sharp hike in next year's rent.

"Jewish people like continuity," I said. "They remember everything and want to tell their children about it. Pass it on. No matter where they live." I was being boring and pleasing and not making any headway in finding Myra or diving deeper into the plane blow-up.

"Oh! Yeah! Big time!" Nat had decided to enjoy himself as he folded his shirt on the ironing board. "They have stories going back to the forty years they spent wandering around in the desert. They've been settlin' all these years all over the place and tellin' stories."

"Talking about settling down, let's eat," Mrs. Meeropol said.

She had made filet mignon, beet salad with red onions and goat cheese, steamed asparagus, and grilled potatoes. Nat and I devoured it all with hardly a sound. She picked up the thread when the silence was unmistakable. Nat had no time for what she would have to say.

He finished his dessert and picked up the tabloid from the coffee table and took it away into his room. For the rest of the evening he breezed by, going from room to room, launching flying comments on everything and anything we discussed. I noticed he was collecting clothes and throwing them on his bed in the room at the end of the corridor.

"Where you going?" I asked him.

"Just a trip," he said, without looking at me.

A trip? Like down the rapids? Like a boat trip? A plane trip? A hike? Like what's the fucking mystery here? I decided not to push. A time would come when he'd choose to tell me. His mother felt the tension rising as he kept running about, acting as if he were too busy to give either of us the time of day.

"What made your late husband start the business with gravestones?" I asked.

"Oh, it was in the family! My grandpa was doing it in Brooklyn, you know. Moshe's grandfather had started one in Newark, but he gave up and started a shop on Canal Street selling Swiss watches, pens, and jewellery. Moshe's father was an expert with marble, a stone carver. Not a bad one." She said "bad" like a long, stretched-out word. Baaaade. I liked that. "He stuck to it. Persevered. But we figured Montreal would be good. Also, I was learning Hebrew and we came here on a visit and the school had no teachers, the old lady from Poland having died. Imagine! So my mother got that job, besides doing her needle trade business. Now I'm past seventy and Moshe's gone! Who'd a believed it?" Her eyes watered and she looked away towards the bookshelves.

Sometimes when I had dinner with them, she'd give me a bigger piece of wild salmon than she gave Nat. He'd say, "See! That's not 'cause you're a guest. That's 'cause she thinks you're a surrogate son." But it didn't faze her. She'd wink at me and tell Nat my mom would do the same.

I felt this connection with her because she didn't conceal her fondness for me. Perhaps I was too involved in what was not my business. Perhaps I should be censured for asking questions about an émigré history that wasn't my own. Perhaps. But his mother enjoyed spending her lonely nights telling me stories that no one else would listen to. Moreover, she incited in me a reason to question everything like my grandfather did.

As far as the Myra situation went, I didn't discuss it that night, although I had intended to. I trudged home fingering the same scraps of paper in my pocket, seventeen different clues all carefully fondled, all vying for a brief flirtation with my curious fingers. Perhaps, I thought, if I didn't pay equal attention to each clue then the murderer would slip away, or the tango dancer would disappear.

The moon slid by the sulphated copper dome of another heritage building renovated beyond rescue. The smell of beer and pizza wafted past me and into the open mouth of the Alfred Hitchcock painted on an alley wall at the end of a cul-de-sac. Someone passing by gave me a shove and didn't say *pardon,* but by the time I turned around he was gone so I mumbled a low *sonofabitch.* No one heard. I said *sonofabitch* again, but only in my head this time.

Why hadn't he told me where he was going? There are partitions in his head. Makeshift corridors that he knows how to negotiate. I remain a coiled viper. Lying lazy and motionless. I do not react even when my anger is building up. I hiss inside.

CHAPTER EIGHT

Finally, Ms. Banks

She was there on a Wednesday afternoon, sitting on the outside stairs to my apartment, legs crossed. I was coming back from work, the sky was clear and blue. Her face was partially framed by the geraniums planted by the landlord. I could see she wore those large sunglasses graded from dark to light, top to bottom. I noticed her torn fishnet stockings. Black. The sun caressed her mourning legs while casting long shadows from the houses on the other side of the street. I walked slowly up to her and leaned against the railing. She was looking down the street and hadn't seen me coming. She turned, a bit surprised, and then said, "So how'd you figure out it was me?"

"I guessed, but I wasn't sure," I said, with a cool that I was beginning to cultivate. "I knew Nat had something to do with it, so I put two and two together."

"That Malia is Myra?" she asked coldly.

"Yeah." I smiled pleasantly.

"Well, she isn't!" She was dead serious. "But that's another story." She looked away. "How 'bout coffee? You can treat. Your reputation won't go down the tubes, you know what I mean? Or don't you wanna be seen with me? Well, I'm not goin' away from these stairs. I will sit here till you do something."

I fidgeted a bit. Did not say anything.

"Are you incapable of reacting?"

She fired away, smug and self-contented. Skipping over the obvious and going straight for the jugular. Or, like a child in an elevator, she simply liked to press all the buttons. She hoped to set off fire alarms, stir up problems, and throw it all in the air like debris. She liked strife. I felt awkward beneath her onslaught, but my brain didn't send any signals to my mouth. She carried on.

"Ah! I see. You want me to say sorry for gettin' upset, is that it? But I did what I did, you know, for the right reasons, so I won't!"

She put her hand out delicately, like she was offering it for a polite shake. I pulled her up with enough force that she stood on her heels, hobbled a bit, and then gave me a kiss on each cheek. There was no alcohol on her breath, but there were remnants of a flowery perfume mixed with sweat.

"My place or the pub?" I asked, without any trace of nervousness.

"Why would I be waiting here if we were going to go to a pub?" she shot back. We climbed the stairs to the second floor. I had cleaned up my two rooms and even the kitchen. I had actually bought a new flat panel and mounted it on the wall. My place looked good. The desk and the computer table were a mess, however, as I had been writing and printing. I asked her to make herself comfortable and then went to tidy, gathering the papers and putting a large architectural magazine on top. "No need to clean up," she said, "I'm not here trying to pry. Do you know why I'm here?"

I sensed that she was more prepared to defend than I was prepared to attack. In a way that was good, because I wasn't about to let myself be raked over again. Had she realized she had gone overboard?

"I figured you thought it over, after you got my email explaining the mishap, and that you believed me." I cleared my throat to continue. "And then Nat must have given you my address, so you decided to walk over rather than send me an email. I appreciate that."

Nat figured in every conversation, in every move I made.

"Whoa! Whoa! Whoa! Not so fast! I did have second thoughts, but I still felt that you had jerked me around by not turning up. I actually went and saw Mrs. Karamanlis two days after I got your email. She said it was all true, that she had screwed up and left the wrong room number with her dumb-ass nephew. So, yes, finally, I felt that I shouldn't have dumped on you. In all honesty, I felt like making it up to you. I scared the shit out of her, I think, and she didn't bring up the smashed mirror." She crossed her legs, totally self-assured.

"But the question I have," I said, "is how you knew it was me, the same person as at the chiropractor's? Did Nat set it up?"

"Of course, he did! How many Chuck Bhatts are there in town? And besides, I knew your name from the office file. Nat said a lot of things about you that I liked. And I knew that I had planted a seed in your head about the plane and Trois-Pistoles. Up there! It's true, isn't it? And you're a writer, right? I got you thinking!"

"I try to write, yes. I have brandy, Jameson, some Merlot and maybe a few beers. What would you like?" I felt measured and in control. I knew she was watching my every move.

"I said coffee, didn't I?" Her testiness wasn't going away, but I was ready to take her on. She had crossed her arms over her chest. I was tensile, stretching myself. Trying to be easy, all over. But, somewhere I felt that if there was one more provocation, I'd throw her out of my apartment. Maybe. There was an impossible sweetness in her.

"Okay! So, coffee it shall be." I went over to the kitchen counter and started a brew. I returned and sat on the couch opposite her. I noticed, with her shades off, that she had dark patches under her eyes. She noticed as well.

"Don't worry, I've been sleeping well, but I need to sleep more!" And she laughed. "Now we have two ways to start this conversation. We can talk about the tango, or we can talk about Trois-Pistoles and Myra. Which is it?"

I noticed she didn't bring up Malia. "I'd like to know Malia better." This seemed to annoy her, so I continued, "But I'd also like to know what you feel about Dr. Roberge and why he took off for the Caribbean. You know there's something about Linda St-Onge and her death that really bothers me. Something smells bad, so I checked some things out, and I discovered stuff I'd like to share with you." She stared at me earnestly.

"Well," she said, "I think he was planning the trip for a while. I overheard stuff. He had made a few trips while I was still working for him and the second lady he married, Jacops or something, she came by a few times. They were seeing each other long before Linda died. By the way, did Nat tell you that I was a hooker or something like that? Actually, I'm not."

Out of the blue! She had said this with her head down, looking at her fingernails.

"No, he never said such a thing. Why would he? He said you're serious about getting into acting, although he felt that you let people give you a reputation you didn't deserve."

I would have explained further, but she interrupted.

"Wait a minute! So, he brought up the issue himself—or did you—the hooker thing?"

"He said some folks in the neighbourhood saw you differently than you were and he was annoyed by it."

"He's a decent guy, Nat. Sometimes overconfident but . . . he's also at a loss and doesn't know what to do, you know what I mean?" She said this looking straight into my eyes.

"Actually, I don't know what you mean, but are you saying that you're at a loss and don't know what to do?" I held her gaze.

"Of course, who isn't? Aren't you?"

"No. I work three or four days a week and then I write and hang around the pubs. I'm not at a loss. Did Nat tell you I was writing short stories about the Main?" I covered my lack of confidence well. The conversation was going nowhere. I returned to the kitchen to prepare the coffee for her in a large mug. I put it on a tray with a few cookies, sugar, and a little pot of milk. She looked at it and asked if I had anything savoury. I went back to my little pantry closet and found some cheese sticks. She was hungry.

"I like these! These are good. I like salty cheddar." She settled down and ate several as she sipped her coffee. "Nat told me you've been a close buddy of his for a long time, since high school, that he trusted you, and that you were a serious sort of guy who worked on things until you finished them. That was meant as a compliment you know. He really feels close to you."

"Anything else?" I asked. The compliments were beside the point.

"Well, he said you'd like to see me for some special reasons and it made me curious. So he gave me your email address but I wanted to play it safe. You never know what kind of weirdo you're dealing with."

I assured her that there were plenty of those around here. I told her that I had wanted to see her because after we'd met the second time she told me how the chiro was married to the heiress and that his ex-wife, the painter, had died in a plane crash. "It stirred something in me and I couldn't sleep."

"Go away! You couldn't sleep?"

"There was something about it I couldn't quite put my finger on."

"Is that why you so desperately wanted to see me?" She asked without any mischief in her eyes. She sipped the coffee and looked up at me as a child might. This girl needed to be hugged and yet I was not ready to do it.

I walked over to a couch opposite her and sat on the arm. I slowly told her, in a low-keyed manner, what I had found out in my library searches. I explained how I thought that a woman with large shades and a Benz idling outside had handed me the bomb that blew up the plane in which Linda St. Onge was flying. She stared at me for a few seconds and I felt something volcanic building up in her and then she exploded.

"Fuck! Fuck! Fuck! Are you serious?" She jumped up, came over, and put her hands around my shoulders. I was a bit taken aback and felt awkward. I am generally awkward and don't know what to do with my hands in such situations.

"Oh my God! What's going to happen? You know what I mean? Oh my God! Are you going to do something? Fuck! Does Nat know? Oh my God! Cold-ass bitch! I saw her go into the doc's office so many times! No wonder! Shit! Now, I won't sleep tonight. That's it. Look what you've done to me! How am I going to sleep tonight?"

"I'm not sure it was her. Maybe someone she set up."

"Oh it was her! I know for sure!" Her voice went hoarse as she said it.

She went on like that, repeating "Fuck! Fuck! Fuck!" mechanically and pacing around the coffee table. Then she went back to the couch. I got up and stood against the kitchen counter, not knowing what to say or do next. I felt guilty about precipitating this frenzied situation, but I felt good about it, too.

I tried to present myself as calm, serious, and not at all distracted by her attractiveness, although my inherent stiffness began to bother me. I looked through the parting of the white curtain on my kitchen window towards my neighbour's balcony. She had put a bougainvillea in a white pot and the flowers poured over the edge in a reddish pink cascade. An effusive unrestrained overflow. It calmed me.

"But you know, you can't let this slide. I mean, she can't . . . well, they both can't get away with it." There was the wild attractiveness. The sublime conviction.

I wondered if I should show her the photocopies of my findings in the library, but she was already too anxious, and I wanted her to settle down. It was at that point she stood up abruptly, went to the washroom, and didn't return. I started to wonder what to do. I asked if she was okay. No answer. Eventually she emerged, looking tidied and refreshed. She put her arms around me and gave me a hug and said, "Don't worry. I won't discuss it with no one and if there's any way you want me to help, just give me a shout."

"I'd like your help," I said. "Can you stay for a while?"

She looked at the black dial on her watch and said, "I have to be home."

"Can I walk you there?"

It turned out she lived in a two-room apartment off Avenue du Mont-Royal. I accompanied her to the front door. She gave me a long hug and kissed me on both cheeks, then asked if I still needed a chiro. I told her my back was stronger. She turned to go up the stairs but then swivelled back, came down the stairs, and put her arms around me and squeezed the area at the bottom of my backbone. "Sherlock," she quipped, "I'm with you on this one." She laughed out loud. Her laughter resonated in that noisy street.

I had finally met Myra Banks. My spirits lifted. I hadn't set up an appointment to meet her again, nor had I taken down her telephone number, but we knew where to find each other. It was only a question of time. The coils of tension in me were stretching out, seeking a free state. Good God! I wanted to sin right there and then. I mean I felt released, abandoned, unrestricted, unashamed, and energized. I wanted to ride out on a horse, coattails flying, hooves barely grazing the ground. I would pull out and point the tip of my sword with enormous zeal and desire at that target of evil and injustice that I was ready to pierce and knock to the ground. With the same intensity that had been missing in my life for so long.

CHAPTER NINE

Blown from the Inside

A week later, I reached home and found an envelope tucked under my door. In it was a cut-out from a newspaper with a picture of Corinthe Gabriel-Jacops. Myra had attached a short note: "Take a good look—that's her without the shades—the parcel bearer. Love, M."

M, eh?

I stared at the picture, briefly locked in fear as I looked into her eyes. I wasn't sure if that was the face I remembered. But the picture was helpful, and 'M' was on board. I flipped open my laptop and continued searching the Internet, scouring the newspapers or websites dealing with the Bas-Saint-Laurent region. Whenever I found anything even vaguely connected to the issue, I'd cut and paste it into a directory file entitled Trois-Pistoles Cold Case, or TPCC for short. That evening, I found a new item on a website dedicated to local news in Rivière-du-Loup, dated almost a year earlier, reported by one Jacques Belanger.

Apparently, a local fisherman named Rejean Bolduc had taken his boat to tour the island of Notre-Dame-de-Sept-Douleurs and had recovered several metallic pieces he thought must have come from a sunken vessel. Both parts, however, seemed to show signs of severe burning. Bolduc had taken one of the pieces to the local pastor Charles Gagnon who had served in the Second World War as an engineer in the Ferry Command, and who also had a keen interest in local history. Reverend Gagnon had doubted the pieces were from a boat.

The next morning, I managed to reach the website by phone and asked to speak to Jacques Belanger. They told me he had left the area, having moved to Vancouver almost a year ago. When pressed, they insisted they had no contact with him. I gave them my contact information and made a quick note that I stuck on the corkboard next to my desk: Boat or plane? Charles Gagnon?

Two weeks later I was surprised to find a long email from Jacques Belanger himself. He had, of course, been contacted by the protocol-savvy paper.

Dear Mr. Bhatt,

I believe you've been looking for me. Unfortunately, I'm in Caracas for the next few months.

In relation to your inquiries, I did have an extensive chat with Reverend Gagnon regarding the discovered pieces and wrote a feature piece for a Montreal paper based on the recorded interview. However, the paper seemed to lose interest after requesting several edits. I am attaching the unpublished piece. However, more pertinent, are the following quotes transcribed from the original meeting with Reverend Gagnon. They form the basis of the material redacted from the article.

Transcript: "The fisherman Bolduc actually recovered two pieces. One was from the sea, entangled in his net, but the other, believe it or not, was found almost five kilometres inland, close to his house. If he had not seen the first piece, he might have ignored the second, for if you look at both pieces you'll notice they are identical, although inverse. They are both sections of the floor of the cargo hold, one from the right, one from the left. If you look at the holes in them you will notice that they were both blown out from the inside, like the petals of a flower. And yet the investigating team declared that the plane most likely had engine failure while caught in a crosswind and plunged into the water. If it had plunged into the water the bodies would have been recoverable intact, but only body fragments were recovered."

Transcript: "The plane must have encountered a catastrophic decompression after an explosion. It exploded in the air over land and the perimeter of fragmentation is more likely over land than sea. I believe there are many parts still lying out there on the land waiting to be retrieved. A postman making deliveries reported he had heard a very loud crack in the skies at the exact time of the plane's supposed mechanical failure, but that he was behind a row of houses and couldn't see anything. No one recorded his testimony, and yet everyone knows he was an honest man who would not make this up."

Transcript: "Forensic examination of destroyed objects are fundamental to understanding a crime scene. It is critical to understand what type of explosive might have been used and to spectrally analyse the remnants for chemical traces and spikes. No such activity was undertaken on the pieces discovered when the small plane crashed over Trois-Pistoles. Was there a flight data recorder? No independent body—as required by the International Civil Aviation Organization—investigated the incident."

Transcript: "It was left to the RCMP and the SQ to close the book on that case. There were no survivors and out of some 16,000 parts that belonged to the plane, only some fifty pieces were recovered. The arc of recovery was arbitrarily reduced, confining it to a limited area over the waterway. The efforts at recovery were abandoned early."

Reverend Gagnon was aged and feeble at the time I spoke to him, but there was no mistaking the sharpness of his mind. I enjoyed our encounter. He had served in the Canadian forces during WWII in Europe and had a strong technical background. He spoke English as fluently as any Englishman in Montreal but with better grammar. He had prepared for the interview and chose every word for its clarity and accuracy.

He was not excited, nor demonstrative, but spoke as if simply doing his job as a responsible man of the cloth, seeking justice in the facts.

Mr. Bhatt, I am very relieved that someone has revived interest in this cold case. I believe the Reverend is still around and you may want to talk to him. If there is anything I can do, please let me know.

Sincerely,

Jacques Belanger,

Caracas, Venezuela.

CHAPTER TEN

Two Reflections

On my way home I picked up avocados, tomatoes, eggs, milk, mango juice, and sourdough bread at the corner market run by a Tamil family. When I reached home there was a note stuck to my mailbox. I took it and went upstairs to my apartment. The note said "Call me. 514 980 4246. Malia."

Why was she Malia again?

I put the food away, changed out of my office clothes, washed up, and called. She never even said hello. "Can you come over right now?"

"Of course."

It takes about ten minutes. In my mind, I rehearsed what lay ahead. I'd remain collected, in control, and would glide through whatever might happen. Thank God there was no Mrs. Karamanlis involved. With every step, I felt my resolution build. I also tried not to step on the cracks in the sidewalk, having persuaded myself, as a child, that it's preferable for one's feet not to fall on any of the fine brass dividers cemented in the pavement. It was a meaningless superstitious game. Such was the tension she could induce.

The door opened slowly. She stood in front of me in a long black skirt with the hem on one side lifted nearly to her shoulders. Her hair had been raised in two peaks. Her lips, like a crimson sunset, were on fire. Her lace blouse was the same scarlet. Her cheeks were rouged. A blue light shone behind her, casting long shadows. She didn't smile as she looked me steadily in the eye. As I stepped in, she put her arms out. I entered them to give her a hug but she dropped her arms, swung her skirt like a matador and then raised them again around my neck; her eyes closed, her lips almost touching mine. Then she opened her eyes and kissed me gently, before leading me into her living room.

There was a lamp on either side of the room, no rugs, and little furniture. She walked over to a CD player on a shelf and punched a button. A tango started. She lifted her arms again and this time held me gracefully. I knew a little bit of tango, so that helped me along in the beginning, quite speechless. Suddenly she whirled around, kicked a leg out and wrapped it around me as if we had been doing this forever. Out of my league, fluid and flawless, she leaned back, arching. She neither spoke nor smiled. She had it all choreographed and went about it as if driven, her head thrown back, her face whipping from side to side, whisking me around as if I were a life-sized rag doll. Then she looked down to the floor, fitted her whole mid-section into mine, and led me in a vigorous trot towards the wall only to stop at the last possible moment. I felt awkward but overwhelmed.

After ten minutes, the music ended and she gave me a hug, took a rather curt bow and led me to the couch, next to one of the lamps. I sat down, still holding the palm of her hand. She slowly released herself and went to the side table where she had placed two glasses and a bottle of red wine. She poured and then returned to me with an *"Enchanté!"*

"Are we going to talk?" I asked, looking at her lips—red poppies ready to burst—and trying to sound concerned. "I thought from your note that something was wrong."

"We had planned to dance, hadn't we?" There was a hint of a smile. She noticed me staring at her lips and brought them closer to mine. Then she put them softly against my neck and slipped her left palm inside the open section of my shirt, resting it gently on my collarbone. Her fingers wandered and loosened the top button of my shirt. I could feel her moist tongue begin to lick my upper lip gently before she raised herself on the couch and wrapped herself around me in a firm and flower-scented embrace. With her knees between my legs, she held my head and kissed me slowly. I put my arms around her and held her—every single muscle in her body was coiled like a spring. I ran my hand down her back and then towards the inside of her thighs. She was muscular, supple, and warm. Her body responded to my touch in waves and her lips began to travel. Tremors ran though her body and collided with tremors in me. She looked into my eyes.

The aroma of desire, the audacity of the unspoken, the wanting, had peaked. She unveiled her breast. It quivered as I ran my lips over her brown nipples and the warm palm of her hand slid down. My shoulder blades curved around and nearly touched as I held my breath and she ran her lips over me. Everything that followed was without words. There were occasional cries that sounded like deep calls for release.

Then we lay on the couch, our arms tight about each other. She rested her head on my shoulder and briefly fell into a light sleep. When she opened her eyes, I put my finger on her nose and was about to ask a question when she put her finger to her lips and said "Shhh!" She rose and went to the kitchen to bring back grapes and more wine. Every time I tried to start a conversation, she put her fingers to my lips to silence me. She put her arms around me and again put her face on my shoulder. I sensed that her body was again tightening. After a while she looked up at me and I realized she'd been crying. My shoulder was moist from her tears. Then she got up abruptly.

She walked to her bedroom and returned in fifteen minutes, dressed in her usual skirt and blouse, looking like someone else. The rouge was gone. The hair hung loose around her shoulders. There were reflections of her on the window; one on the inside window and one on the outside. She said with a glowing smile, "Well hello there, Chuck! How are we doing?"

I must have hesitated as she right away got testy and added, "So, what now, are we going to talk or what?" I wasn't mystified any longer. I finally got it. Malia was not Myra. Myra was not Malia. They were different! Chuck had finally got it!

That night I invited Myra to a small Italian restaurant just north of Jean-Talon. We walked all the way up St-Laurent, taking about twenty minutes. We kept no particular pace, just ambling along, the way tired torsos walk freely. She didn't hold my hand. We chatted all the way about Linda St. Onge; not about her paintings, but to develop an incursionary foray, a plan of attack. A commando operation into the core of the frozen case.

At the restaurant, she ordered a boring prosciutto and melon appetizer and sipped a martini. I had a glass of whisky with no ice and a superb mozzarella cheese ball with a light batter and a sharp red dressing, whose name made no sense to me. Sounded like a battle cry. Like in a war zone with golden tomatoes being sliced in the air and dripping slowly down. We smiled but didn't touch. We both pounced on our racks of lamb and, feeling pretty stuffed, skipped the desert. I walked her back to her apartment. With a wistful look on her face she said, "Thank you, Mr. Bhatt."

I had her telephone number now, but did not ask when we'd meet again. I felt I couldn't, as if it was presumptive.

I did manage to say, "Please call me sometime. I am listed as Chuck Bhattacharya."

She turned and left. She didn't call for several weeks and I pursued the cold case of the St-Onge murder alone. Needless to say, the sudden and long intervals between her appearances had taken on a different meaning in my life. It gave me confidence. A sense of single-minded purpose. A self-sufficiency that was absent until now. The fog hung high. With clearances, like holes of hope. Indecision, hesitancy was something I relied on. I had pulled back always. Making weighty considerations, whereas others sprang into action. I was now fortified by the clearances. I was in a position, now to decide.

CHAPTER ELEVEN

Khyber, No One Passes

My grandfather had not been keeping well. He suffered from a chronic cough. Nor was my grandmother working at my parents' restaurant. She had a knee problem and it was too hard for her to stay standing while kneading the dough for the *rotis*. My father bought an industrial-size dough maker to replace her and he found it did the job, quicker. Effectively, my father had shafted my grandmother. Retrenched.

My parents remained very busy. My mother managed the business administratively while my father experimented with the menu. In the *Summer Review,* he was mentioned as one of the city's most innovative chefs. The restaurant itself looked great. My mother had redesigned the menu as well as the interior. She had placed a steel counter around the bar, stainless steel lamps along the walls, and not a sign remained of Taj Mahal-style archways or elephants running wild along the headboards.

All this to explain that when I needed to talk it made good sense to bypass my parents and head directly to the grandparents, who had moved to a two-bedroom condominium with a large balcony near the Lachine Canal.

I must have walked in looking a bit down. My grandfather immediately perked up. "Ah! I see storm clouds!" We sat down to chat, but he treated the occasion as if we were preparing to climb a great mountain, attempting to break through the hovering fog and on to where things were calm and safe. My grandmother brought us a bowl of chips and two beers, informed me she had started to take swimming lessons at the local pool, and left.

My grandfather asked about "Nathuram," the fascist Gandhi-killer. I told him Nat was struggling in his acting career and I hadn't seen him for a while. I added, though, that he seemed to be maintaining himself in good physical shape. "Maybe," I surmised, "he has a new girlfriend."

"He visited us, you know. We had a long chat."

"Really? Nat was here?"

"Yes, for several hours. Asking questions. About Afghanistan. He also brought some Muscat wine, which he knows I like."

I was mystified. Nat had visited my grandparents, on his own, in their new place? It was nice that he had brought over the bottle of wine, but why? Then I realized that I had been over to visit his mom and taken her Armenian sweets my mother had made. Nothing unusual there. But it wasn't like Nat. He wasn't a chatterer. He was a doer.

My grandpa was revolted by the war in Afghanistan. Maybe he had driven the conversation to its unusual length, wanting to vent? Had Nat merely been a convenient outlet for his streaming opinions? It was possible. These inferences went by me in the first nanosecond. I had come to discuss Myra, or Malia, or both, to gather the wisdom my grandfather might offer regarding the weird and wonderful feelings she caused in me. I was a transforming nerd looking for mentoring—but mostly courage. My grandfather gently tolerated it. However, he only wanted, once again, to talk about Afghanistan.

"I told your friend that Canada had no reason to be there except to play second fiddle to the United States."

"Where?" I was distracted.

"In Kandahar!" he said. And he continued, while he wheezed in a disturbing way.

"I explained to him the real reason. The Tories believe that military spending provides employment, jobs, and industrial growth. That's cow manure, you know." The filmy skin on one side of his face quivered. "This is all about the guilt of not having fought in Iraq. Do you really think young men and women are being sent off to die because this government thinks there are terrorists in the hills and caves of Afghanistan planning to attack us? Rubbish! This Afghan war has no meaning for Canada's young. None. Besides, the more you bomb their hills, the more terrorists you grow in our cities. The fellows who carried out the attacks weren't living in caves. They were living in France, England, Germany, and elsewhere, before they came legally to the United States." He said all this with great energy, enjoying his beer. I noticed, however, the wheezing was increasing. I looked again at the filmy side of his face. *What really did that to him? He had never actually told me.*

He pointed to a picture perched on one side of his desk that I knew well. It was a faded grey shot of a massive gate, like a mini Arc de Triomphe, with a rickety tin sign hanging on it that said 'Khyber Pass'. Under it were men in long Afghan tunics wearing huge headgear standing beside a few mules. They had Enfield rifles slung on their backs. A few had daggers visible beneath their tunics.

He used to show me the same picture when I was a kid, telling me that the people who lived there wouldn't let anybody pass if they hadn't come in peace. 'The Khyber Pass', he'd repeat ominously, eyebrows raised. In West End High when I did a presentation on Afghanistan—I don't know why I chose Afghanistan—I, too, raised my eyebrows while telling the whole class that no one would pass through those gates unless they came in peace. My teacher, Mr. Leblanc, was suitably impressed and gave me high marks. From then on, he called me *Khyber Pass* when we met in the corridor. I liked that, considering it respectful, not derisive.

Nat had attended my high school presentation and asked a lot of smart questions. I had even taken him back to meet my grandfather to further discuss the subject. That was years ago. But now, for some unexplained reason, he had come again, and this time on his own.

"No one will win against a mountain tribal people," my grandfather was saying. "They fight generation after generation, hidden away in the mountains, swooping down with fresh waves of their children until, exhausted, you find no reason to continue."

"So, it's a lost cause?" I said. "Try convincing the media."

"You won't beat them. No helicopters, drones, missiles, MANPADS, or Hummers will defeat them. They'll sit in their caves and snipe away at you one by one, and if at night you're not careful, they'll come down to slit your throat and hang your head from a post for everyone to see."

He pulled out a map from inside an old National Geographic and put his finger down on it firmly. "Here, in this pass, in a village called Daar, they make every kind of gun you can imagine. They even made antique guns like Gatlings if that's what makes you happy. Otherwise, they make AK47s, Uzis, Mausers, Brownings, Glocks, you name it. Anything that makes you happy!" He laughed and wheezed simultaneously. "There are lathes in every hut and little kids hammering out cartridges before loading them with gunpowder; I tell you, they're ready to meet any army, which is what the Soviets learned when the Afghans started trading poppies to buy shoulder launched missiles and turned the Pass into a tank cemetery. For us to pretend we're on the side of a just cause is sheer folly. Everything that the Americans have brought in there from pancake makers and toilets to baseball bats and Coleman stoves will be packed up in 53-foot containers and shipped back or simply melted down by the Taliban. By the way, how is work going?"

I ignored that particular question and started on about Myra, telling him that she was a very attractive but eccentric person. He listened patiently and then said, "It's important to have friends who are stable." He went to get another beer for each of us. He was, I knew, thinking things through.

"What did you mean by 'stable'?" I asked as he returned.

"You know, there comes a certain point in time when you can't blame the things that don't turn out right on your parents." He said this looking at me. I thought he was going to bring up my dad, but he didn't. He actually meant it in a more general sense.

"There used to be a time when parents controlled everything the child did right up to college and even beyond. If you were from an upper-class family and your parents were well educated they'd set the standards and you'd follow, like getting into good colleges, fighting for scholarships, all of that. It's not like that anymore. Nowadays kids are more influenced by their friends. They've developed this strange notion that parents are an accidental happening, something that gets in the way, an impediment to independence. Social workers talk about broken homes but don't seem to understand that society itself is broken. It's society that sets standards nowadays."

"What's your point?" I asked.

"Well, you'd mentioned that Myra wanted to be an actress and that you felt she turned hot and cold, on and off." I had described her that way. But it also occurred to me that Nat might have suggested certain ideas about her to him.

"People don't want attention just for the sake of it. They want to be loved because maybe they never got the attention they needed. So, the child seeks a kind of loving attention when they're older. Now if they've been loved and taken care of when they were kids, then there would be no real reason for them to be unstable. So, if she's being hot and cold, it's because she's trying out different roles. It has to do with social mores. In her mind, she is testing the waters. She wants to be sure, probably because she has no one to fall back on." For sure, Nat had spoken to him.

Having said that, he began to cough. I waited for him to settle down. He looked pale. "That's what led her to become an actress, a profession where she's encouraged to walk in and out of roles, each on a trial basis. You said she's the daughter of a well-known critic, didn't you? You said she doesn't get along with her mother and her father has been long gone, yes? So, I think she missed out on a few things in life and doesn't feel stable or doesn't even know what stability means. Her interests may not be yours."

My grandfather was no doubt from another generation, but his observations struck me as worth considering. I didn't want to argue with him on any finer points or try to make too much of it, either.

I walked all the way downtown from the canal and passed by my parents' restaurant. I looked in and saw my father greeting people, a smile on his face, tilting his head to the side and pleasing the entire world with the affected, maudlin ways of a charming, humble, Eastern man, which he was not. I chose not to enter. I finally relented and took the subway at the student-infested Guy-Concordia station, riding it toward the toilet-walled, destitute, and homeless St-Laurent station. I emerged, turned the corner and started for home. In the distance, I clearly saw two women stomping down opposite sides of the street. One wore a black dress that shimmered shapelessly. She was moving away from me. The other wore a white jacket and large sunglasses, and she was striding gauntly towards me.

CHAPTER TWELVE

Things to Do

Suddenly winter had cut loose after an indifferent summer. Blistering winds curved your back. The streets were twig strewn, ice-bound, nearly abandoned, and the day was frigid, bone dry. The sun streamed down on the black ice, deceptive and dangerous. Dried dog poop emerged out of hollow pockets in the dirty ice. With hands tucked inside, I stepped carefully over the marbled surface. I was headed towards the Meeropol home again. She asked me to come over. She had something to say. Important. She seemed happy to see me.

I'm not sure people ever reveal their true intentions, even to their best friends. And how honest can one be with words, anyhow? Maybe they're only ever chosen tactically, to distract or redirect; assuming one doesn't simply remain silent. She told me Nat had been away for a few days in New York, and maybe had landed a contract. I felt happy for him, but couldn't hold it in any longer. "Mrs. Meeropol, is he going out with someone?" It was my grandpa who had planted that thought. I asked it as casually as I could but, still, I saw that it surprised her. She laughed a bit too noisily and said, "Chuck, if I knew you'd have known before me, no?" Then she stared at me, sensing something was wrong. I knew, too, that something had changed.

A few weeks earlier, Nat and I had run into each other. When I asked how he was, all he said was "Things to do, stuff." A breach was building, a greying of space between us. He was holding back and remaining distant, preferring to pretend he was always in a rush. I agree that how-are-yous are often mechanical, inconsequential. But replying "things to do" meant worse. He wasn't willing to disclose or discuss. Besides, his use of words like 'things' and 'stuff' riled me. A twenty-year camaraderie was on the ropes for no apparent reason.

She had asked me to come in, but it seemed like she was not really coming clean. Whenever I went to visit it wasn't only to look him up, but also to listen to her, so we began a conversation about the two bagel shops on St-Viateur and Fairmont streets. It was enough to briefly light up her face. "Hey!" And was I startled. "Did you know there was a time when people believed they were the same store? Like connected underground. The bagels were exactly the same. Some of my friends said that their basements must be connected under the street with an underground tunnel! Can you imagine? So naïve! But it wasn't true. We know that because when the telephone people dug up the street we could all see that there were only pipes, no secret corridor. But imagining it was fun!"

Then she told me that the omelettes at Baby's were not like when the store had started, around the time of the war. "Anybody who knew how to flip an omelette at home knew how to throw in green pepper, grated cheese and onions and make the mishmash. No big deal, really. It was the feel of the diner that everyone liked." We talked about the Euro Deli and how she and her husband had often gone there. Then she suddenly looked away and I noticed she was wringing her hands very gently. She became interested in the designs on the carpet under the coffee table.

"I don't want to bother you, Mrs. Meeropol. I'll leave now. Do you know when Nat will be back?"

"No! No! Don't go. I want to tell you something." She disappeared to put the kettle on. She knew how much I loved tea. She had even bought Makaibari Silver Tip Darjeeling from one of the new tea houses on Sherbrooke. I had told her my father served that brand.

I often perused Nat's books, so I walked over to the shelf and started looking for anything new. I'd seen them all before: a history of NY Living Theatre, plays by Boal and Fo. He had a political side to him. But no flash. We had seen a few plays together. Yet, as he said about agitprop, "You ain't goin' to make a dime out of it, bro', because the folks who go to theatre aren't the ones who'll man the barricades!"

I noticed a few envelopes, two rings, and a watch on his desk. Beside the lamp I saw a pair of sunglasses. They seemed familiar, but not Nat's style. I walked back to my chair and saw Mrs. Meeropol standing in the doorway with a cup of tea in her hands, watching me. Her face was long and beautiful. My grandfather once told me he liked Ava Gardner, that she was a true star—gracious, beautiful, and far from a bimbo. He said she was intelligent. I imagined that Mrs. Meeropol was a lot like her. I walked up to her and she handed me the tea. I sat down and started to sip while she fetched crackers and cheese.

Then she sat next to me and asked, "You were looking at the sunglasses, weren't you? You know whose they are?"

Then, yes, I knew. I took another sip and lied. "No, I don't. Looks like they could be a woman's." She hadn't put any milk in the tea, the way I liked it. You don't mix Darjeeling with milk. It's light and delicate. You can mix milk with Assam teas because they have lots of body. They're blended like Scotch. But Darjeeling is a single malt, as RK would say.

"Yes, they are. This girl, Myra, has been coming to see him. I think I should tell you because Nat said to me that . . . "

I didn't let her finish, even though I was trembling inside. "I wish he'd told me. Thank you for letting me know."

Now I knew why he'd been avoiding me, why he whizzed by on his bike only to wave and disappear. I had understood his distance as his way of concentrating on his stumbling career. I had wanted to give him all the distance he needed. I had assumed he was still seeing Nathalie from Merise's bar. I had assumed wrong.

I finished the cup of tea and said I had to go home. I left Mrs. Meeropol standing at the top of the stairs as I gently closed the door.

I was disgusted. My whole body felt infested, wormed-up. Every step of the way I felt betrayed, detested, done in. Nat and Myra. Nothing meant much to either. Bullies! Everything was made up, appearances only. Images flashed by, from the first day I had met her, to our tango tryst, and the encounter after.

I walked home talking out loud. Every step I took, it felt like the air hung me up. As if I could not get my foot down to the pavement, as if I had lost contact with the street I thought I knew so well. When I passed by the Copa, the barman Rudy shouted out, "Wazzup!"

I totally ignored him. He hollered after me, "Hey! Chuck! Wazza matter with ya?!" I didn't turn. I was so mad that nothing mattered anymore.

I didn't want to go home and slump onto my couch alone. Nor did I want to go to a pub and drown in alcohol. I wanted to think rationally and stay stable, like my grandfather suggested. They were the same fucking sunglasses she had worn when she sat outside my house. She could have just as easily left them behind at my place. So, she left them at his—what was the big deal? She'd known him longer than she knew me.

But Mrs. Meeropol had let it all out—hadn't she—like she was part of the understanding. He was her son, so why should she feel sorry for me? Suddenly Ava Gardner looked a lot more like Meryl Streep; an evil, scheming, conniving woman wearing Prada, not the woman I had imagined. And all for that miserable son of a bitch who had swooped down on Myra, ready to do anything to promote his failing, disoriented, fucked-up life.

At least I had a job.

For the next several days I was a zombie at work, moving in a daze, unable to understand what I was doing. At home, I ate whatever I found until the fridge was empty. I refused to cook. I spent a week walking the Main from evening till late at night, only coming back to my apartment when exhausted, collapsing on the couch in front of the droning television until I fell asleep.

Then one night the doorbell rang, sounding like a hoarse fire alarm and travelled through my body like an electric wave. It went all the way up and then all the way down, from my head to my toes, vibrating my entire length. Never before had the doorbell rung with such brutality. It threw me off the couch and I rolled over before standing unsteadily. The clock on the TV said 1 a.m. I peered through the peephole. Nat didn't say a word, just stepped in and sat down. The TV had been left on and he quietly went to turn it off, and then settled on the chair opposite me.

"I wanna straighten this out with you." He slumped down on the couch and stared at me. "I know what my mom told you." He began confidently enough, while I remained faint inside, nervous and ready to explode. But he'd been such a close friend; I really was not ready to take him out.

"I have nothing to say," I managed in a slow whisper.

He considered that silently. "My mom knows shit, okay? Actually, you should have a lot to say when you hear what I have to say. And you have to believe me."

"Oh, yeah." I said, "Fuck that, man! Are you going to tell me that you had no choice?"

"Chuck, it wasn't like that." He was calm but I had no intention of letting him off easy. He carried on. "I told Myra that you were my friend from high school and I could never go behind your back. She told me there was nothing happening between her and you."

"She said that? Incredible! Was it a fucking fantasy then? I mean, really!"

"We went for dinner once and . . . yeah." He hesitated.

"Okay! Don't need the gory details. Your mom told me enough."

"My mom knows nothing, man! Nothing! Myra came over one of the nights actually to talk about you and started getting playful, like, you know, and mom saw that and because she feels about you like she does, as if you were a second son or something, she gave me shit. And that was it!"

Suddenly I felt sorry for Mrs. Meeropol, a.k.a Meryl Streep/Ava Gardner.

He continued, "But something weird happened last night. She was walking down Mont-Royal and was wearing this black dress, like she was going for a tango class or something."

"That's how she looked when I went to her place." I bowed my head and shivered.

"Exactly! The woman you know, Chuck, that you're in love with, is not Myra Banks."

"What do you mean?"

"Because when I went up to her she didn't recognize me. Ignored me totally. She walked right by me and I ran back up to her and she told me to shoo, to get away, to fuck off! She kept walking down the street like she'd never known me. Her cheeks were red with rouge and she was wearing fiery lipstick with a red silk scarf wrapped around her neck."

"What the hell are you trying to say? That she didn't want to talk to you?"

"No, she didn't recognize me, man! Like she had never met me! She was walking straight ahead and wouldn't even look at my face and finally when I touched her arm she whipped around and glared at me like I was some kind of a hobo. She said "Mister! If you come near me I'll call the police right away!" I backed off.

"This was not Myra, man. It was someone else." He looked genuinely sad.

"And what did you do?" I was beginning to believe him.

"I just stood there and folks walked by thinking I must be a retard. You know, I think something is wrong with her. Really wrong." He looked at the rug under my coffee table and I stared at him. "Listen," he said, after his moment of silence, "I'm not going to fuck you over for this girl or anybody else. Okay? My mom got it wrong and I am not gonna bother straightening it out with her. Myra asked about you more than talking about anything else."

"And she told you that she was not seeing me? Is that right?" I wanted him to confirm it one more time.

"Yeah! I told her, 'Look, Myra, Chuck's my best buddy. Be nice.' And she said that she'd just met you once in your apartment because she wanted to clear things up. She repeated she wasn't seeing you. I'm not interested in her, man. I like her, like we had a nice dinner once, as I said, but that's it. There's something wrong with the girl. You can buy that or not. But that's the damn truth."

"She seems kind of distracted and exciting. But I can't find her, when I want to. You know, she and her mom slip into an alternate world. They have split personalities. Like they switch in and out. I don't know. That's my guess. Like her Mom did stuff out of an uncontrollable instinct. She played games. Myra may have been affected by it. She took it on as a lifestyle. She normalized her dual life."

Nat left soon after. I closed the door behind him and fell onto the couch. The phone rang at 3 a.m. but I didn't answer it.

Icicles had formed in the eaves outside my window. Looking in. Short daggers of imprecise, unformulated decrees, verdicts. A cold Montreal dawn was sliding through the ill-fitted, uninsulated guillotine windows and slipping in a poltergeist shadow. The wind had crept in and had chosen to wait in the corner of the room, like a cat with a cloak. When I woke up, my hands were chilled. I touched my stomach where it was warm and rolled over. I was there and it was not a delusion?

CHAPTER THIRTEEN

On Board

Next night, sounds came up the stairs. Crossing the door in the corridor. Hard heels against creaky wooden stairs. Beads of panic. Slipping down my forehead. The storm trooper walked through my door wearing sunglasses. She was already inside before I could get out of my bed. It was in the middle of the night—the grim clanging of a diesel motor was heard loud in the alley downstairs. Her adjutants were outside in a phalange of cars, arms crossed, waiting to take me away. The über-topmost stomped in and entered my room and removed her long leather gloves. She stood at the foot of the bed for a few seconds and then leapt over the frame and landed with her knees on my hips. I did not cringe. I was paralyzed. I looked at her carefully, at the tone on her skin, when she opened her mouth and said something that I barely understood. Her lips pouted and her knees jarred into my midriff. It sounded barely like a threat but done with a red smile and a dark eye that scanned my face with contemptuous sensuality. I tried to hold her off by the shoulders and her powdery-flowery smell, like in a funeral home, rushed into my face. My hands went through the air. She whispered into my ears as her steel-cold teeth bit my earlobes. She said she knew where I was headed and understood my plan. A wind whistled through my body, cold-barrelled into my bones. I was moaning and I knew that.

I sprung up, shivering, and was awake. I went to the fridge and drank cold water, looking behind me in the glow from the refrigerator light. I swallowed the water, the hair on my neck curling up as if an electro-magnetic wave from a far-off tundra had crossed through my apartment. I lay down, awake for the rest of the night.

This was not the only time. Once before she stood at the end of the corridor leading to my washroom. Like a tabloid image caught in a grainy long shot by a paparazzi. It reminded me of the photo from the newspaper cutting Myra had given me.

These visitations were a load I'd have to carry alone. Myra had expressed an interest in helping but wasn't exactly proving reliable. Nat had egged me on but only cared about his own projects. Then there was Myra and Malia. I decided to visit my grandfather again.

"Maybe I should go to the Sûreté and let them know what I've discovered. What d'you think?"

"You'll be handing over an unresolved case of plane sabotage, long forgotten but definitely requiring some intelligent investigation, and exposing yourself to an endless stream of manipulations. It's your choice."

"I could survive that."

"Could you? Eventually someone in the Gabriel-Jacops syndicate will learn about you and your information. God knows what they might do."

"You mean knock me off?"

"Possibly," he replied, and then smiled at me. "More likely the police will decide that you're a crank. They'll listen to you, thank you, and advise you to go home. The case will be re-shelved. How would you like that?"

"I could approach one of the local French-language newspapers, especially the ones that cover the crime scene—talk to one of their well-known journalists, help them with the investigation."

"Sure, and then get shot up in a parking lot for having gone public. What you need to do, if you're serious, is to flush this woman out, get her to make mistakes in public. She's not that sharp. There must be a way under her skin."

"She's been getting under mine. She appears at the foot of my bed at regular intervals."

He laughed and lit his pipe and then released the smoke slowly in front of his face. "Big crimes always leave silly errors. Someone loosens the bolts on all the wheels when it takes only one loose wheel to spin the car at high speed. He is caught on CCTV. The DNA is found in the gloves in the garbage can in the alley. Strychnine traces are left on the bar counter. The flaming tower collapses but traces of fire excitants are discovered in the parking lot below. There are always inadvertent slips and careless conversations which can throw the game open."

Conan Doyle and Le Carré. He continued to brood behind the smoke. He was convincing me to get with it and not cower. That was his style. If I were a nerd, he wouldn't tell me. I was his only grandson. "Come to think of it, it's very perplexing that she mailed the package herself, instead of sending a hired hand to do the job. She may have thought that the fewer people involved, the less potential evidence available. Is that why she did it? Stupid move, I'd say. *Comme ils disent autour d'ici, merde* happens!"

After refreshing his thoughts with a gulp of some Mortlatch that he tucked away in the bookshelf, he looked me in the eye and winked. "You know," he said, "we could work on this together." The idea had occurred to me at about the same time.

I nodded slowly and began to tell him what I had learned from scouring the net, having delved into the corporate reports and online magazines, reading the press releases and tracking the enormously confounding network of holding companies, intertwined operations, and controlling trust funds. Aside from the diamonds and the pulp and paper interests, they had a company that offered 'secure transaction services' for managing 'difficult assets.' Registered offshore, the company also provided legal advice on 'mature asset management.' Corinthe Gabriel-Jacops appeared on the board of seven companies, while her brother Cornell appeared on seventeen. Her brother was the one, apparently, in charge of the mining operations in Africa, as well as the security company. They had companies registered in Mauritius, others on the Cayman Islands, and still others in Florida; yet all were linked with the head office in Montreal. I summed it up: "They've managed to blend the private with the corporate, and the personal with the global."

He asked, "But why did she do it? Why didn't they simply go public with their affair? Why was she in a rush? The super-rich have no need to bump off anyone for insurance money. So why did this happen? And why in such a spectacular manner—blowing up a plane?" He paused before adding, "Had Linda been a part of their operations? And had turned whistle-blower?"

That night I opened my diary and went over my notes carefully, only closing the book in the early hours of the morning.

A month passed and I hadn't seen Myra. I was sitting on my front steps reading the newspaper when she appeared.

"Hello! Thought I'd say hi!"

"So, who are you now? Or who do you want to be, Myra or Malia?"

She didn't say anything but squeezed herself into the tight space next to me. She lifted her shoulders, took a deep breath and ran her fingers through her hair. She looked at me sideways, sighed, and then looked out at the houses across. I returned to reading my newspaper.

"I ran into my father recently," she said.

"Yes? That's good. I didn't know he was around."

"I've been seeing him often."

"How about Nat? Seeing him as well?" I infused the word "seeing" with necessary spite.

She again pushed her fingers through her hair. She closed her eyes for a few seconds, then opened them. "I wanted to see you, but you weren't going to believe me anyway. I want to explain to you that after talking with my father . . . that something broke inside me. Can I talk about it?"

I moved over on the steps, allowing her to sit comfortably.

"Chuck, listen, you gotta hold off before shooting from the hip, you know what I mean?"

"I'm listening," I replied evenly, wondering why she was talking about her father. All the time we'd known each other he hadn't existed. Her mother did, and was sometimes seen in the vicinity, but her father had neither form, image, nor voice. Suddenly, here he was making a grand appearance. A father-bereft girl was now regularly encountering him.

"I had incidents happen to me as a child and I was never sure what they meant. I never talked to anyone about them. They remained closed inside me until I recently met my dad. My childhood—the summers in the Townships—were difficult. I absorbed a lot of stuff from my parents that I wish I hadn't." She lowered her head, as if to think things through.

"Myra, I don't want to fight with you. Nat spoke to me and I'm at peace. It doesn't matter. You don't have to explain yourself." I wasn't sure if I was being too blunt, too concili-atory, or missing the point altogether.

"It's not about Nat."

"Oh?"

"My father explained why he and my mom split up. He didn't know I had seen so much of everything. It hurt him, knowing. I was too young, even though all I saw were images, like watching a movie. But it did me in." Her voice started to break. "I always wanted to be someone else. Like my mother was two people, acting as if she were in a trance, like it was natural to sometimes take on another character. And then, suddenly, I did, too—I became a different character and it was special, so special."

I had some idea where she was headed. I remained silent. She stared ahead. She wasn't trying to lie. There was a story unfolding within her and I was there to listen. I had heard and known enough about childhood trauma to know that living a dual life doesn't come from a schizoid personality; it's enactment, role playing, the thrill of theatre.

"She lived a second life."

"You can tell me what happened, but I find it hard to believe that you'd let it go on for so long, over so many years. Why didn't you do something about it?"

She took my hand and held it in her palm. "I didn't see it as a problem. It was simply who I was. If it weren't for my father, I'd still be doing it. I really believed I could live two lives, as well." She said that staring at the pavement. "My mum was sharing her life with a man, who came by the barn in the country house on Thursday nights. Yes, he came on horseback from some adjoining town. And they would screw their brains out and a friend and I watched from a crack in the window, like it was a TV show. My mother was like a flamenco dancer and the man's chest glistened with sweat from the heat in the summer barn. They did things I could not imagine, and then he would get up and leave. My mother went back to the cottage, turned on a lamp, and started reading a book. The woman in the barn. My mother. The woman in the cottage reading a book, with satisfied composure. My mother. And one day my father turned around and came back early on a Thursday. He would normally come back on Sundays. Until then I thought it was normal, what my mom did."

I looked at her sideways and she raised her head to meet my gaze, eyes glistening. I didn't feel sorry for her. I didn't want to feel sorry for her, either. I was still upset. There would be small mercies only. "So, did you feel attracted to Nat as Myra? And was that all a charade between Malia and me?"

"No!" She looked pained. "I have no attraction to Nat." Then she took a deep breath and, still holding my hand, said, "If I hadn't seen my father, I would never have understood what was going on. You know what I'm saying? What I saw my mother do . . . it was like something that boiled over from time to time, and I couldn't distinguish what was real from what was a dream. But now it's slowly coming clearer. I feel I've been living a phoney existence my entire life. She lived a dual life and I thought that was quite normal. She had flings every weekend with this guy on horseback. I was just eight or nine. They split eventually."

We sat on the stairs in silence. I was convinced that she wasn't lying, that she had seen things that scarred her, but I was having a hard time reconciling that new information with my old anger.

I offered to walk her back to her house. At the doorstep I said, "I don't buy it, not entirely, but I would like to meet your dad someday."

"Why?" she asked.

"I don't know," was all I could say. I guess I was working on instinct. "But there's no future, if I have to deal with two minds in one body."

CHAPTER FOURTEEN

Shadow Pictures

The Commodore is a 100-seat diner located two blocks away from the Jean-Talon market. Myra had chatted up the co-owner of the Commodore without telling him that she'd been fired from Dr. Roberge's quite a while ago. When she told him that the doctor had decamped for a Caribbean island with the missus, he chuckled. Everyone in the right circles knew that the chiropractor had married into a wealthy family after his first wife died in a plane crash.

The restaurant serves French and Italian cuisine, mostly a wide selection of square-plate pizzas and homemade pastas and sausages, all accompanied by superb sauces, white or pesto, garnished with fresh herbs. They also serve Champagne, oysters when in season, sharp cheeses that gently dissolve without sticking to your teeth or the roof of your mouth, and a prudent offering of light wines. They make the greatest salmon tartar in Montreal, with chives, shallots, chopped cilantro, red onions, olive oil, and a dash of lemon and hot pepper. People fork the bounty into their mouths, roll their lips into a wondrous circle, half close their eyes and express their pleasure with whispered, kissing sounds. Even I do it sometimes.

Design-wise, it's faux Mediterranean cool all around, with single roses in crystal vases on each table. There is no hint anywhere of murder, mayhem, or sabotage. There is no hint of disquiet, concern, or even wariness. Smiles abound.

Myra and I ordered a square pizza with white sauce, this time sprinkled with minute pieces of prosciutto, and waited for the co-owner to turn up. Myra knew him. She also knew that Dr. Roberge would slip away at lunch and meet Corinthe Gabriel-Jacops here.

People in this neighbourhood hang out on street corners like rockers. High-end fashion statements—de rigueur. They gather around large concrete flowerpots that the borough has placed on the road to tame the traffic. In fact, everything is forced to slow down here. Fast is not hip and you need to make yourself visible while taking time to acknowledge others. Greetings are mandatory. Even the spit-polished red, black, and yellow Italian cars roll by slowly. Windows roll down and smooth salutations follow. The Ducatis are parked at wild angles, often with engines still running, their colours bursting with summer energy.

The Prada shades, the soft leather boots with the brass buckles, the strapless black gowns, the flaming red stilettos, the white slacks and the striped shirts—all so casual. The shaved heads or GI cuts of the men emphasize the neighbourhood's youth. Hormones, pheromones, adrenaline all nudge, leap, and lunge in blustery confusion down the sidewalks before settling into one of the pricier dining spots. A gentle tip of the head or a long drawn out "Eiiihhhh!" is inevitably followed by fists connecting in the air and then an equally elongated riposte that never concludes in the expected affirmation or question, but rather a general observation on everything that is going down or coming up in the hood. Then follows a casual, "by the way, how's the boss, eh?"—a fleeting inquisition about the missing other half.

Across the street, the man running the espresso bar has faded colour pictures of himself on the front page of a local daily with a now-dead mayor referring to him as a Montreal landmark. It's pasted up on the wall opposite the bar, which is more often run by his bejewelled, heavily tanned, sizable blond daughter. She's in her forties, wears a chiffon black blouse with a plunging front to reveal an acne-scarred cleavage. Once, I remember Nat chatting her up and leaving a fat tip right there. I was taking my time, adding the hot milk slowly to the espresso, writing notes in my diary. When Nat left for the pool table, she asked if he was still doing films. I replied, "Yeah, when he wants to," giving him more credit than he deserved.

Yes, stereotypes abound but the waiters are friendly to the point that you don't know whether they're joking or being grimly serious. There is a deadpan approach, menacing at times, but these guys have it down like they all went through the Joe Pesci and Roberto Benigni School of deadpan emotions: a readymade scowl followed by a wild laugh and a prod into your ribs that makes you double up either in laughter or pain. They are all brilliant actors, capable of long conversations at the slightest provocation. If you ask them to recommend a dish they might begin their answer by describing a specific tamarillo tree in a village in Sicily. If you ask them a personal question, they ask if you're a cop or a lawyer. "What! You a *flic* or somethin'?" If you select an item they recommended, they announce to everyone around that your wife has just declared her unconditional love for him. Since your wife or partner is with you, you feel like a veritable stuffed bell pepper. Other tables respond with howls and cries of their own. Like an operatic movement. Sometimes the chef is hauled into the restaurant by the waiter and accused of serving a fly in the linguini. The waiter insists that the aggrieved patron should not take this lying down.

Everyone looks uncomfortable and confused. The chef, however, promptly announces he is ready to do battle with this nuisance fly, pulls out a swatter and whacks the waiter on the head. The show rolls on.

"Heh! Heh! Heh! Smart guy, that chiro!" said Leo, the co-owner. "What can I do for you, Ms. Myra?"

"Leo, this is my boyfriend, Chuck."

"I can see that, very clearly, from his eyes and yours. No make any mistakes there!" I was amused that she had kindly placed me on her list of known acquaintances. "You like-a your dinner?" he asked me.

"Yes, I loved the pizza. Special!" That was my genuine response.

"You wanna go sit at the bar and chat?" he asked.

We went over to a vacant corner. The barman was cleaning glasses. "Dinner was great. It always is," Myra added with exuberance. "My friend, Chuck, is doing a piece for the newspaper on chiropractors in the city and the type of clientele they have." I was amused by the silly story idea, but also alarmed by how easy it was for her to spin a lie.

Leo left and soon returned with two light dessert wines in tall champagne glasses. "Yeah, your boss, the doctor, came here often. Now, not so much. Sometime for lunch, sometime for dinner." Leo began to expand on his own—"always with that Gabriella woman. They know many of my customers. She comes from a rich family so everyone likes to hang around her, you know? Long before, his first wife, the painter, died in that crash. When she died everyone here already knew he was going to marry this woman. Sometimes God makes life too easy for some. But the poor woman, the painter, she was sort of well known, too, no? One time, we have an incident here, did I tell you?"

"No, what happened?" Myra was all ears.

"Well, she catch them here a-having dinner together. She walk in and stand right at the table. A quiet argument start. Everyone look, so they walk out into the street. Then a big sound and screaming. The painter slap her hard and she, Gabriella, fall to the ground. Dr. Roberge try to help her up and the painter kick her twice in the ribs and walk away to her car. The doctor pay the bill and they leave."

"So that is, like, real! Wow! Did Roberge come back with her after?" Myra asked.

"Sure, many times! After a month they come back. They like my Ossobucco Milanese!" Leo rubbed his chest. We were silent. I wasn't taking any notes, but it occurred to me that an incident like that might be enough motivation for retribution.

"Linda St-Onge," I started, "yeah, she was famous. People knew her well in Quebec art circles. The other one, the one who fell, Corinthe Gabriel-Jacops"—I corrected Leo on her name—"can you tell us more about her? Did she ever come with other friends?"

"Yes, yes. She come here mostly with the doctor, you know, but sometime she come here with friends. Maybe I have picture of her. You see on the walls? Like Pacino there, De Niro, Mr. Big, Angelina, all kinds of people come here, you recognize them? Sometime not good people, though. Yeah. Maybe I find some pictures. You write a social column?" He asked me.

"I just write about the neighbourhood." I, too, could come up with a quick lie, but one at least rooted in some truth.

Leo left for the back office while we sipped our wines, looking at each other and smiling. Myra rested the palm of her hand on mine and I felt she was relaxed. He came back dusting a laminated picture with a napkin. It looked like it had never been hung on the walls. Myra and I pretended not too be too interested, but it took me a hundredth of a second to spot Corinthe sitting at a table laughing with others. My blood went cold.

"Funny, I thought I had a picture of the doctor, but no. None. Just the lady. There she is with Normand St. Maurice, the TV host, and Carolyn St-Jean. And here is someone from the Orlando Cheese family—what's his name? He owned part of a soccer team?"

It was Myra who answered. "Leo, I don't know, but can we borrow this picture? We'll bring it back soon."

"Yeah! Yeah! Sure! Sure! But bring it back, my friend, in the same condition. And don't use in any piece, okay? "

We thanked Leo, finished the wine, and returned to Myra's apartment. I didn't stay long. She kept the picture. She said she'd track down the names of all the people in it.

CHAPTER FIFTEEN

Letter from Hell

Mrs. Meeropol opened the soundless door. There was no creak, no shudder as the door pivoted smoothly around on its hinges. The silence of the opening door was noticeably and ominously predictive. As in "this is just the beginning, my friend, the storm lies ahead." Above, ash was descending from the sky. The two stories were merging. The plane that was atomised and a friend that had soared away into an unknown sky.

"Is everything okay?" I asked timidly.

"Come in." Having said that, she turned and went into the kitchen to make tea, as usual. I sat down on the nearest oval couch, where I always sat down, not knowing where that three-legged device was best supported.

"I know you and Nat put some distance between you, so I guess you don't know. He left last week."

"Where has he gone?" I asked with a raised voice.

"Kandahar, maybe." She said this from the kitchen, her voice distant. Kandahar. Or, Alexander. Where the Greek conqueror had panted to a stop, exhausted—and then was shrugged-off, dismissed and transformed into a hapless has-been by fierce Pashtun pride. A mountainous impenetrable fortress. The word Kandahar, as she stated it, bounced off half-destroyed buildings, snow-capped mountains, colonial archways, and hidden caves; it travelled through long corridors where reapers hid, scythe-ready, behind each column. It was a word formed within the toothless hollows of ancient nomadic mouths. "Kandahar? Kandahar?" I repeated. "He didn't tell me anything."

Afghanistan! Now I knew why he had visited my grandfather. He had been preparing for his new role, doing his research. His body had become that of a panther, sinewy and tight. When he was working out so hard I had thought he was doing it for a specific role, maybe for a movie contract. I had never asked why.

I followed Ava Gardner into the kitchen. She was leaning against the kitchen counter, a teacup and saucer shaking in her hands. I crossed over and gently took them. Two large tears emerged and dribbled down her dry parched cheeks.

"What is he going to do there? Has he joined the Army?" I would have been totally disillusioned if he had done that.

"No. He has a job with a security agency. He's been training with them for a while. I never thought he'd be posted to Afghanistan, but I think he knew. He left this letter for you."

She handed me an envelope. I tucked it into my pocket. "Mrs. Meeropol, is there anything I can do to help you with the business? Do you want me to take care of the accounts?"

"Thank you, Chuck. Drop by when you can."

It was the wrong time to stay for tea. I started towards home, but my impatience to read the letter got the better of me. I detoured and sat down at the Copa and was again greeted by Rudy, the barman.

"Yow! Wazzup, dude? You okay?"

"Cool! Everything's cool. Wazzup with you? A Boreal lite, puullees!" I said it like Obama used to—hanging out with the guys, playing hoop, being cool; the type of thing the media laps up. I was not necessarily in a bad mood. Just developing a swag.

Rudy poured the beer lightning fast and slid it to a stop right in front of me. No foam. "Get you some nuts?"

"Nope, I'm good. Thanks!"

I studied the beer before I took a sip. A waitress passed by and kissed me on the cheeks. "Hey, Chuck!" she chirped. "Been a long time." She spoke like nothing had changed; so the word hadn't spread, no one else knew Nat had left. I had changed. Significantly.

Rudy had a client watching a European Liga game at the other end of the bar. He served him a pint and then came back to me, smiling. "Why'd you give me the shaft the other day, man? You walked by and said zip. Wazzup with that, bro?" He wasn't going to let it slide.

"I was outa sorts. Got some bad news at work." I satisfied him with a lie. He didn't probe any further. I pulled out the letter. He immediately understood I wanted to be left alone. He said, leaving, "As long as Chuck the man is Chuck the man, everything's okay!"

I ripped open the envelope and took a large gulp of the beer.

Hey!

What's a letter like this worth? Zero. No one writes letters these days. Not me for sure. But this one is special. I will write like I have always spoken to you and right away, I gotta apologize man, 'cos I stayed away from you for the past few months. It had nothing to do with Myra. Read on and you will know. I was in intense training. I know you're not going to like what I have to say. Yes, dismiss me! I respect you, man, and nothing will change that. Letters are not my thing. *Words are yours. Mine are feelings. I can express some of them when I'm with you on the Main, walking, chatting, feeling the buzz at night on our little strip, there. I personally thought it was always crap. A forever reinventing itself, continuously bankrupt neighbourhood, full of small-time boring dreamers and poor artists who continue to imagine that they are hip business folks! And I bet you will rip this letter open sitting in a pub or a café, over a pint, right there . . . bitch about me in your head, somewhere between Duluth and Prince Arthur. Am I right?*

I was not getting anywhere with the acting. My agent is a piece of shit! She always got me these stereotype tough guy roles. Enforcers. I'm sick of it. I wasn't asking for a lead role. But maybe something a wee bit more intelligent, man, than a muscleman or a dead-beat cop. Know what I mean? It struck me that it was my physical features that were misleading everyone. I decided to turn the tables. I ran into someone who was looking to hire long-term positions in the security industry for people in good health. Well, there was nothing they could complain about as far as I was concerned. You know how I had been working out. So, I took the bait. I went through training in all sorts of equipment. What really appealed to me was the electronic stuff. I like that. So, after a three-month training period, I am being sent off to Afghanistan to work in the Canadian Trade office in Kandahar. It's right next to the consular offices. They need to have a perimeter defence set up and are subbing all these jobs to private agencies. Yeah, it's not your bag. I have been talking to your grandpa. He was emphatic it was a failed mission. Boy! What a wealth of information he has inside that shiny head of his! Will not, as a nation, get us anywhere. He said that. He is very deep, man. I know where you get it from. I had to consult him. Hope you don't mind.

Anyway, I am leaving. We all need to leave things behind. You need to walk away too. Walk away and start fresh. That way there are surprises. Otherwise you get too familiar with living in the fog. It's a job. I will come out of it with a CV I can show around. Just watch! And by the way, just to finish our half-assed conversation late that night, I didn't have anything physical with her. Now you can believe me, or you can talk to her. I have no reason to jive you, man! Fuck me over in your mind and I know you enough to know it isn't gonna make you feel good. So, love me as you always have, because I will always.

Take care, man! You don't owe me anything. My mother would love to see ya from time to time. She dotes on you. Be back soon, I hope—and will write to you on your home email.

Respect for the brother! N

I must have read the letter seven times before I folded it up and put it back in the envelope and into my pocket. My body shuddered gently and my mind raced around in circles: from idea to emotion, from anger to gratitude, from disbelief to relief, from melancholy to madness. I felt bitter but better, angry and lost, loving and remorseful. I had believed in him but he hadn't believed in me. That was the hard part. He was so totally fucked up! "How could he do this?" I must have hissed under my breath because Rudy looked at me from the other end and nodded his head, politely—like he knew. Why didn't he talk? He had gone secretive and done me wrong; pissing me off, messing with my life, and now he was trying to straighten things out from long distance. That wasn't going to work. No way! Why was he choosing to turn himself into dust?

The sliding doors of the bar were slightly open, allowing in a dry, cool air. I looked out into the streets. The lamplights cast a pall. I looked instinctively down the street. He was not careening away on his bike. I looked again. There was no one hanging around with a coffee cup or a cap held out. They always tipped their hats to him. He was gone. They had withdrawn.

Rudy slid me another pint and wiped the counter. I stared into it. Yellow, piss-coloured liquid, shaped by the alluring curve of the glass, a mocking profile of a modish night—lights bouncing off the rim, reflecting the short black dresses and skin tones of a trendy night outside; the dark stillness of a disinfected street in a city with no caves, no long beards, no turbans, no long tunics, no gunfire, no ambushes, no cares. The fizz from the beer rose anxiously and popped into the barely hygienic air above it. Had he signed off, or had he signed on to something I'd never realized was in him?

I followed, Nat led. Nat brawled, I tried my best to control him. Sometimes I got mad at him for going out of control. I read like a nerd. He avoided reading and instead asked questions and stored his answers, mentally. One time, he beat up a bunch of rogues in a nightclub line for harassing Luc, the panhandler. He stepped in and cleared the whole line-up before the bouncers even knew what had happened. He walked away as soon as the cops arrived, and even stared down at them. I was nervous as hell, ready to throw up. Nat rolled up his sleeves, nodded his head, and said to me, "Don't stand around, you'll get busted. When the pigs have no clue what they are doing, they will arrest you for resisting arrest." At a school concert, the teacher asked him to play Perfidia on guitar, because he was good at the twangy style, on an old Les Paul with reverb on a small amplifier. He insisted on playing Apache, like it was played by Link Wray. The teacher said, *No! Perfidia!* And that was it. He was adamant about playing Apache. And he did it. I played rhythm guitar with him. The school kids were up on their feet when he ended by playing a nasty, mean D chord that made the speakers crack and warble and when we finished, he pointed to me. I basked in his style. No other friends mattered. I had to get on with this cold case. He had sent me a clear signal.

I walked home thinking about Nat. Was he doing security detail somewhere in Kandahar? I mean, what exactly was he doing? Was he walking on a dusty trail protecting a Canadian business investor seeking road and hospital contracts? However I approached the subject of him in Afghanistan, I could never find an answer to the question I most wanted to ask: why had he left so quietly?

CHAPTER SIXTEEN

African Diamonds

Myra called the next evening to ask that I meet her dad, Gerry. There was a bird in her voice. She had shown him the picture and he had immediately recognized a character sitting at the back. It was Derek Boswell. The name meant nothing to me, but Myra's dad was about to set me straight. Nothing could replace Nat as far as ground intel was concerned on the hood, but I felt a sense of ease that this Gerry had come into our midst. I was not always sure that I could handle this project without Nat. It was reassuring, now.

Gerry had moved onto the Main and was working in an office on the second floor of a building near the corner of Duluth. It had recently been renovated by the city and now housed a number of small NGOs: architectural firms, design studios, and film companies, none of which seemed to need more than a room or two. He worked for a non-profit company that provided computers to schools in Africa.

I was greeted with a firm handshake and a gaze looking straight at me. I liked him immediately. He had stylish grey hair along the sides and a thick dark crop on top. He wore a dark blazer and a collarless shirt. He was both the administrator and the spokesperson. He took my jacket and hung it up next to his. Mine looked limp in comparison to his.

"Myra was telling me about your project. I've looked into their company. It's big-time operations. Their foreign ops make the domestic one look like a store front. Alice in Cinderella's garden." He smiled confidently.

I had some clue what he meant by that. He spoke like a Soviet-era cold war sleuth. He spoke in riddles but with conviction and had a gravelly voice that added serious enigma.

He continued, "However, that the daughter of a Montreal scion could be involved personally is bewildering at first, but not impossible. She had reached a point where money and resources made her oblivious to the limits of her actions. And the family's enthusiasm about 'clean diamonds' makes things curious. They never are. Take it from me. Any outfit working in the mines in Africa is operating, at best, in a grey area. They hire local mercenaries as enforcers, engage in deals with rebel groups, pay off government officials, and rely on the services of political gangsters. This is unavoidable. No African diamonds are bloodless."

He said all this with the characteristic sanguinity that he had already established. He invited us to sit around a table in the middle of one of his two rooms, as if at a strategy meeting. "But look, no one is going to blow up a plane merely out of a personal vendetta or jealousy. That's psychotic, like a bad-ass daytime soap opera."

I listened to him, quite enthralled.

"There has to be a greater purpose to such an event. Did Myra tell you I recognized Derek Boswell?"

"She did, but it doesn't mean anything to me."

"He's a former insurance broker, probably still in jail at present. I would call him the essence of sleaze in this city."

"And what's his link with Corinthe?"

"I don't know, but there was a time when unduly ambitious insurance brokers were raking in millions selling insurance to lonely elderly folks while promising to look after their port-folios, all the while arranging to be on the payout list at their death. He was one of them. Nothing so illegal, just offering a professional financial service. Until he became impatient enough to hasten the deaths of a few of the senior citizens."

"Oh! God!" Myra's eyes widened.

"It gets even more complicated," Gerry continued. "He had been a close buddy of one of the full patch members of the Bandoleers, a rival group to the Shawinigan chapter of the Angels. They helped him in his enterprise. But while he was being prosecuted for the deaths of six senior citizens he decided to turn informer on his previous associates and received a reduced sentence for cooperating."

First big breakthrough. The sun shades, the rushed atti-tude, the Benz idling outside and now she is thick with the hoods. Did Linda find out? All fitted in. My grandfather was right.

But I was a bit confused, too. "Nobody keeps the com-pany of biker gangs if you want to be clean. Absolutely no one. And once you've become associated, you're cooked. Forever on a watch list. How could the police have missed such connections to Corinthe?"

My question hung there, unanswered.

Myra had brought the picture and I began to look at it again, carefully this time. I saw there were two characters visible just outside the restaurant, each of them with arms crossed.

"Who are they?" I asked.

"I imagine they're lookouts," Gerry answered. I would find out soon.

Myra said softly as she looked at Corinthe's image, "We're coming after you! Bitch! Soon! And Dr. Jekyll, we'll ream yer arse too!" She could be sweet and funny.

We began to methodically discuss all the evidence we had, and all the evidence we didn't have, trying to devise a workable plan and evenly distributing the work yet to be done. This thrilled Myra. She was happy with our 'team approach,' as she enthusiastically called it. I'm sure Nat would have said that there is some naivety to all this. But with Gerry on board, it felt better.

She volunteered to trace Dr. Roberge's contacts, collecting all the information she could about his friends and acquaintances and, wherever possible, visiting them. She was looking to pick up information about his habits and behaviour both before and after the murder. She was going to find out how much Linda knew. She even suggested that maybe her paintings had some clues about what she knew. "Behavioural patterns matter," she offered, smiling. "Sometimes the paintings are metaphors." Charming statements.

Her father was to deepen his investigations into the corporate web, especially related to its African activities. The key was to figure out how she got the explosives. He was also to prepare his contacts in the media for the revelations to come. His responsibility wasn't only to help resolve the cold case, but to time and co-ordinate its eventual exposure. He thought ahead.

I had the riskiest path forward, everyone agreed. I'd attempt to get hired at the Enterprise and meet Corinthe. I knew that despite the fact the couple had announced their move to the Caribbean, Corinthe was still a director in charge of Human Resources and lived in town. At the end of each month she'd fly away to the islands for a week. It was my job to confirm she was the woman who had delivered the package, and then to get current pictures and a handwriting sample. For that, I needed to get close. Because blowing up a plane, just because of a slap on the face, was not going to go down too well with the jury.

The Gabriel-Jacops head office is located at the corner of Berri and Rene-Levesque. The granite-faced obelisk has a large diamond crystal logo adorning the gaunt, two-storey portal. The facade of the building has a shine, unlike the concrete buildings surrounding it. There are no windows on the first two floors. On the third floor are large windows. One can only imagine the administrators moving around behind the darkly tinted glass.

A CTV Business Hour program available online had given me more information about the eighty-five-year-old founder. Robert Jacops, still on the Board although no longer the CEO, had patiently insisted how the diamonds they handled were bloodless. "We never deal in conflict diamonds." The program ended with Kelly Patrick, the business reporter, doing his best to define the global abrasives and grinding tools market while explaining the stunning rise within it of a small enterprise originally founded in a remote corner of Quebec. Everything about the company's unexpected northwards performance trajectory was presented as miraculous, legitimate, and hard earned.

As I stepped into the building I saw closed circuit cameras swivelling noiselessly along the top edge of the black polished mosaic on the back wall. I imagined there were other cameras within the tinted glass boxes on either side of the front desk. The receptionist had me sign the log book before providing me with a visitor's badge and asking me to sit.

I put my back to the cameras and began to leaf through a selection of industry journals laid out in a rack below a large oil portrait of the big man himself. A group of Chinese businessmen came in and quickly registered at the front desk. They were immediately badged up and whisked away. I waited for nearly fifteen minutes before someone came to fetch me for my interview in the Logistics department.

The position was for a Shipping Administrator in one of their outlets in Montreal East. The interview was hurried and direct. I was offered the position right there and then. I had no hesitation and accepted.

I resigned from my position at the courier company, which was a sad event. I had worked there for so long and was leaving behind folks who had confided in me about everything: their affairs, their parents' dementia, and their arrogant neighbours who threw bricks at clothes lines whose pulleys screeched excessively. I knew about the bruises they didn't choose to discuss, about brothers who were acting strange and sisters who were coming home late, about being half-Algonquin and half-Quebecois and getting short shrift in both communities. I knew their opinions on the inevitable issues of Quebec sovereignty, *les autres, les raëlians,* and streets destroyed in winter by the same contractors who restored them in summer with lousy asphalt. I knew about their ten-hour waits in hospital emergency rooms and the beaches they enjoyed in Cancun or Florida. I loved my colleagues and they admired what they saw as my even temperament and good upbringing.

Now I was imprudently taking a job to pursue a case, not a career, amongst a set of unknown people, and entering it with deception and intrigue on my mind. The pay would be better, but I'd have to work five days a week. And I would be walking to work. There'd be less time to write. I realized for a short-lived moment that eventually this is how people move out of the Main; one by one the ties get cut. How they cut through the fog. Do people really move out, or do they just take the Main with them?

There was a small farewell party for me at the office during my last afternoon. It was nice. The folks were kind, smiling, and a bit teary-eyed. Some remembered coming to me to settle issues about geography, country capitals, food habits, best sellers, bad movie reviews, what was at the Louvre and not at the Prado, carbon emissions, and other "intellectual stuff." I had, they said, played the role of the bard, the knowledgeable one.

This was a bit embarrassing, because if it were not for RK, my world would not have really expanded beyond the artery that ran north-south on the island of Montreal from the rapids in the north to the Old Port to the south. I stayed late, cleared my desk, explained to the appropriate people the idiosyncrasies I had developed managing the paperwork. Then I made photocopies of the waybill from the lady who, years ago, had entered with what she claimed was a package of dried flowers and left her beastly and impatient Benz idling outside like an exterminating Marie-Antoinette who had no endurance for the peasants who got in her way. I finally left at 7 p.m. on a Thursday evening. From now on, I would be working in the belly.

My grandfather, when informed of the change, said that it was due to an auspicious confluence in the *nakshatra*, by which he meant it was destined by an alignment of the stars that provided succour to those who believe in that kind of thing. I didn't, nor did my grandfather, usually. But then he added an interesting caveat. "Due to your commitment," he said, "the *nakshatra* will take note of the fact that you are taking a direct risk by entering the mouth of the beast."

CHAPTER SEVENTEEN

Puffs of Smoke

I finished dinner and began arranging old papers while watching TV. Breaking headlines began to crawl along the bottom of the screen. Four Canadians had been killed by 'friendly fire' near Kandahar. My stomach turned into a knot. I went on the Internet and found the following news item from an American press agency.

Bombing Accident Kills Four Canadian Soldiers in Afghanistan

WASHINGTON—Four Canadian soldiers were killed early today and eight others seriously injured when a U.S. fighter jet dropped at least one 500-pound bomb on their position near Kandahar, Afghanistan, Canadian defence officials said.

Details are sketchy, but U.S. Central Command officials confirmed a U.S. Air National Guard F-16 fighter dropped "one or two" laser-guided bombs on the Canadians at about 1:55 a.m. local time. Command officials did not speculate as to the cause of the accident, but said an investigation will be conducted.

The Canadian troops were conducting a live-fire night exercise near Kandahar. "Without a doubt there was a mis-

identification of the Canadians and what they were doing on the ground," Gen. Ray Lavoie, chief of the Canadian Defence Staff, told reporters in Ottawa.

The U.S. Secretary of Defense Donald Rumsfeld issued a statement today expressing his "deep regret and sadness over the tragic accident." He said he assured his Canadian counterpart of Central Command's full cooperation in the investigation.

The Canadian Prime Minister said that President Bush called him to offer condolences and also to assure U.S. cooperation in the investigation.

My first reaction was to call his mother, but I didn't. If something had happened and they had notified her then she'd call me. Or would she? I suddenly found myself putting on a jacket, slipping my feet into a pair of old comfortable casuals, and walking out the door. I received a call on my cellphone just as I reached the corner of Duluth and St-Laurent. Horror gripped me as I saw her number pop up on my screen. I answered 'hello' in a very soft tone. There was a perplexing silence for a few seconds; the night went cold, all sounds ceased and the silent words in the sky above became icicles hanging down like daggers. I was sure something had gone wrong.

"It's not him."

I actually stopped walking and threw my arms up. "I was just coming over to your place. Can I?" I said this with so much relief that she sensed it.

"Of course, dear!" She said this as a mom would. I was over at her place in no time. She had an embracing smile and held her arms stretched out to greet me. She gave me a hug and I told her, "I'm so happy to see you." She nodded her head and her lips quivered.

I showed her the printout from the Internet site, and she said that Nat had called, fearing she would panic. He was safe, she said, although the incident happened very close to him. "He sounded angry. I have never heard him so angry about the Americans." I watched her closely as she rose to go towards the kitchen to make tea. There were no physical kinks, no hesitation, no favouring of the hips or the knees. She was agile, smooth, and dexterous.

Although it was late, she was in a mood to chat. "You know," she said, apologetically, "you offered to help sometimes, and I'd be happy if you dropped by. I don't think I need a lot of help with the business. It's already set up. We don't need to market anything, and there's a young fellow that Moshe trained who handles the orders well."

I didn't quite understand, then, why she might need me, with everything all set up, but perhaps she wanted me to drop by from time to time to chat. I sensed that. Did she have no other family or friends? It was past midnight and I was unsure what I should say, so I asked how she felt about Nat having left so suddenly. "Was it planned? Had you known for a long time? Had he discussed it with you?"

She wrung her hands and went silent. I didn't push. I understood. He had deceived us both.

But then, he had at least written a letter to me before leaving. That made a difference. We loved each other, he and I. We had grown up together, walked home from school together, and then suddenly he had disappeared. Now here I was sitting in front of his mother, alone, late at night and both of us seemed paralyzed. She didn't comment on Nat's sudden departure, but instead returned to talking about the business.

"You know, Moshe's death was totally unexpected." She hesitated. "He was a quiet man who went away quietly. But to just lie down on the pavement on St-Laurent and die, unnoticed, and in front of where he had carried on his business for decades . . . "

"That really bothered me," I said spontaneously, thinking of the uncaring hustlers who were taking over the neighbourhood. "No one stopped."

"For weeks I didn't know what had hit me. I knew you were with Nat most of the time. But there was no one with me. I was alone."

"I understand, Mrs. Meeropol. I wasn't sure what was appropriate. I didn't wish to intrude."

"Yes, yes of course." Some hurt there. But she continued. "Even though we're very well known in the community, we haven't been that religious or observant. Nor have we been too forthcoming about our views. I'm telling you all this because you may be wondering why you didn't see a lot of people in the house."

"But there were public condolence meetings and a lot in the press."

"Oh! Of course, Moshe was a stalwart. He was quietly there for so many others, but he just stood at the back. When I could, I joined him. We didn't raise our voices. We didn't make a fuss when there were all sorts of debates and discussions going on."

"He seemed a quiet man."

"Yes, maybe aloof is a better word, which I admired. Making tombstones was not a religious commitment for us. It was a way of making a living. We respected the religious laws but that was about it. We didn't preach, nor did we profess. Our feelings about our religion and our people were confined to quiet nights of discussion amongst ourselves, unravelling things that few in the community wanted to discuss."

She took a deep breath and smiled in a very gentle, attractive way, her eyelids barely holding together as she looked at me.

"You know, headstones were not meant to be ornamental like they are nowadays. It was not Moshe's style. It wasn't our style. You see, Jews are supposed to be humble and attentive, not arrogant and talkative. Headstones are not statements. They are remembrances. In the beginning, headstones were put flat over the grave to protect the body from jackals, or to warn passers-by of the rising spirits. They were not meant to be ostentatious. Even the idea of marking the day of birth and the day of death was foreign to us as Jews. Didn't some rabbi say it was an insult to the dead to put ornaments and decorations over them, that the pious should be remembered for their words and deeds? It was not a tradition in the Middle East to build ornamental tombstones. It was more Greek and Roman. But now, things have changed."

Sometimes when people have thought something through and yet haven't had the opportunity to discuss it, it comes tumbling out in a rush. I thought to myself, how fortunate I am to listen and learn from this lady. But I also felt angry that there was no one else to hear. I didn't look at my watch. It would insult and disorient her.

"I shudder when people request outrageous headstones. It's not done! But what can you do? You try to persuade them." She looked at me and I sensed there were still unspoken thoughts on her mind. I could see that she and Moshe had sat down and quietly chatted about their clients and their behaviour. I realize they had shared a quiet and reflective sobriety, and she was missing it.

"People come here and order from samples they've seen on the web or in some American catalogue. Moshe would try to gently persuade them otherwise, but most were so sure of themselves that it was a lost case. We complied with a smile. And you know . . . when you saw Moshe hunched over his desk with a gentle smile, who could not overpower him?"

She looked at me and saw that my eyes were tired. She asked if I'd like another decaffeinated green tea. I said yes because I liked listening. She made it and returned, then picked up where she had left off.

That night, she told me about many of the buildings on Boulevard St-Laurent and who had owned them. Some of the original families still owned a few of the buildings but didn't live there anymore. They were rented out. There was so much history in those buildings: it was an obscenity that the current crop of shops, boutiques, and parlours operated in such ignorance of where they were. There was no anger or resignation in her eyes, just a profound belief that all that is said and repeated accounts for only a small part of what is embodied within the community.

"Something is always lost when people move, and history gets reinvented, you know what I mean?" She smiled demurely.

It sounded like she was concluding her thoughts, and yet still there was something held back. It was about three in the morning and my eyes had started to glow. She asked if I wanted to lie down in Nat's bed. I kind of jumped up to leave, but she also got up and held me by the shoulders and said, "Stay."

There was something in the way she said it.

I took my shoes off and lay down on the couch and she brought me a pillow and a duvet and covered me. I said, "Thank you, Ava Gardner." She hesitated for a second and then smiled. She understood. She knew I thought of her as a beautiful person with a beautiful mind, and that I adored her. I closed my eyes.

In the morning, as my eyes opened, I noticed her standing by the couch with a cup of tea in her hands. I knew she had been gazing at me. I sat up and said quietly but cheerfully,

"Good morning." I looked into Nat's bedroom before I left. I stood there thinking of the smoke rising from hilltops in Kandahar, the puffs of smouldering anger as elders lit up their stoves and gathered around the glowing heat. I imagined them tearing into day-old pieces of stone-baked bread while the younger ones drew ambush plans with twigs on the reddish soil, their Kalashnikovs on their laps.

CHAPTER EIGHTEEN

Kandahar will Devour Us

Winter had now settled in comfortably again.

During the Friday afternoon, a snowstorm swept through the city like a spirit singing, pushing its way past the tall buildings, through the alleys, dumping tons of fine star-shine in neatly sculptured banks at every corner. The drifts swirled and lifted and stayed on second and third floor window sills, which made the houses in the Mile End district look like square-jawed brown faces, grim with greying moustaches and droopy white eyebrows. The temperature dropped below -9C and stayed there. Tall Hassidic men walked by at acute angles. They braved the biting wind as icy flakes came down like fine spears launched from dark clouds. They clutched their hats while curling locks flew about their ears. Their kids trailed them with their long white socks and faint looks. Everyone moved at the same angle, leaning into the wind.

As it turned to night, the wind calmed. The half-moon sat like a cat perched on the clouds, cuddled and glowing and the snow-covered branches reached into the evening sky like a thousand open palms with long manicured nails. Myra and I talked by phone and decided to stroll through the snow before dining out, meeting at my place first.

I was ready to go when she arrived, but she rushed upstairs to show off her clothes beneath her winter coat. She wore a black lace blouse and the silk shawl I had given her wrapped about her neck in a smart knot. We kissed. I told her she looked like Frida, as in Kahlo, with her dark eyebrows elegantly coiffed. She seemed pleased. She had just gotten two acting stints, so was in the money and joyously confident. She said, "I'm paying tonight. Let's go to your parents' place, okay?"

We trudged through the heavy snow. As we walked by the clubs on St-Laurent, acid remixes of Tribe Called Quest pumped out with hungry bursts of tenor and bass and a beat box that went Digidigipampamparra . . . The people in the bars, with silk shirts open at the neck, behind the big glass windows sat hunched under xenon lamps on high red stools downing glasses of red and looked out at us struggling. Finally I flagged down a lonesome cab and we hopped inside. Myra reached her hand out to me and I held it gently. I thought it wise to initiate a conversation about the food that awaited us, saying that my parents didn't always get it right; there might be a problem with consistency.

"That's true of the best restaurants," she replied gaily. "If you visit any good restaurant twice in a row and order the same dishes you'd probably be disappointed. Anyhow, the place has great reviews."

My mother was there to meet us. Although we speak frequently, I hadn't seen her for a long time. She embraced both of us warmly. My father didn't seem to be around. "I have something for you, stranger!" she said with one eyebrow raised. "Remind me when you're leaving." I had told my mom about Myra when I made the reservation, but she had promptly replied that my grandfather had already informed them of everything. In other words, there was an implied reprimand for discussing the girlfriend with the grandfather and not the parents.

We began by ordering a light Indian beer atrociously named Taj. Then I asked my mother what she recommended. She promptly suggested special items that weren't on the menu. Myra smiled and said, "Ain't nothing like being related to the chef!"

We started with large shrimps—they call them tiger prawns in India—soaked in vodka and roasted lightly in lemon, pepper, and a chili paste with diced onions, all floating in butter. My mother surrounded the prawns with neat swirls of avocado mousse. That was a hit. She had also developed a finely chopped dry lamb recipe, which she recommended to us. It was New Zealand lamb soaked in *dopiaza*-style sauce served with finely chopped onions and garlic with coriander and green onions on the side. It was very dry and dark. We had that with *kulcha* naans. Then she brought us a fish dish. I am sure if my father or grandfather were around she'd have been reprimanded for having the fish after the meat—not done in Bengal. In any case, the fish serving was one of my father's recent developments: tilapia soaked in lemon and the Indian mustard called *kasundi*, covered with coconut cream, wrapped in banana leaves and steamed. She also gave us potatoes and zucchini cooked in a poppy seed sauce as a side dish. My parents, I realized, made confident forays into areas where few Indian restaurants ventured.

Myra noticed a nearby table looking at the menu to figure out which dishes we were ordering. The waiter, a Nepali man, eventually explained to them that I was the boss's son and our dishes weren't available. Not one to treat special privileges lightly, Myra smacked her lips while deftly unfolding the steaming banana leaves. I was amused by the torrent of vivacious energy with which she downed her dinner while ensuring that everyone in the room realized how satisfying she found it.

The snowstorm picked up and a reconfiguration of drifts swirled past the windows. I looked out at it all. Nat was somewhere far away in the mountains while his mother sat with folded hands staring at the lamp outside his bedroom window.

As we were leaving, I reminded my mother she had something for me. It turned out to be a box of CDs I'd been looking for. She'd found them stored in an old Chinese chest used for winter sweaters. She also gave me a sweater—I must have been fifteen when I wore it last—even though she knew it wouldn't fit. Perhaps it was her way of reminding me of the boy I had been. I gave her a large hug that brought tears to her eyes. She quickly wiped them away. I promised to come by more often.

Every time I say goodbye to my parents, even though I live in the same city, I hear a song with lyrics that say this is not the way it used to be, or was meant to be, either.

Myra and I returned to my place. I pulled out the brandy from a shelf in the kitchen and poured it into two snifters. She looked at me and cradled hers in both hands. I saw her lips thorough the glass while she looked over the edge with wide eyes. She had a quizzical look that was at the same time apprehensive and guilty.

"You don't think he left because he was in love with me, do you?"

How the fuck was I to answer such an unwanted question? Even though his letter had clearly stated it was not so, I wasn't sure about it myself. Just then my bedroom radio switched on as it normally did at this hour. Joe Cocker, hoarsely obtuse, aphorizing away that there were too many rivers to cross. I went to my room and slapped the radio shut. Then I remained there, standing against the warm radiator.

She called out to me. "Chuck, please come out. You're just standing there, doing nothing. I know that." When I eventually returned, she was lying down on the couch with her arms out. I smiled. I understood. I came and lay next to her. I placed my head on her black blouse right near the nape of her neck and kissed her. She smiled and then rolled over and held my head with the palm of her hands, very firmly. I closed my eyes and inside me I felt a rip. I didn't know what was behind it and why it was happening to me. I could smell Myra and her chest was resting against mine. There was a warm glow emanating from her skin. It looked so polished, as if a thin layer of cream had been softly spread over it. Then she opened her lips and very gently slid them over my mouth. I smelled the wine, her perfume, and a faint wisp of Indian foods.

I felt every part of her body firmly against me. She moved her mouth slowly all over my face and I put my arms around her. I knew I loved her, but I was also far away climbing a rock-strewn cliff where the wind had stopped and I was alone with no one around. Looking directly at me she said, "Kandahar will devour our lives. You'll see."

Her lips and her words will stay with me for a long time. When she said "our lives," I knew she meant more than the three of us.

Her lips continued to move over mine, the tip of her tongue barely grazing over my mouth. The oxygen was sparse. I didn't feel right. Something felt foreign, distant, and even unwelcome. No doubt I was still upset. The serpent had begun to coil. She sensed it and didn't persist.

We went to the bedroom, but the air was like a cast iron reservoir, a bottomless tank. When she fell asleep from the weariness of Merlot and brandy, I climbed out of the tank and slipped away quietly to sit in the living room with another glass. I pulled out my diary and started writing.

I heard Myra snoring softly in the next room. I wanted to explain my loss to her as she lay asleep—that woman with the two names, two red lips, two looks and two perfumes—who insisted that she was not Spanish and who could totally surprise me by saying that Kandahar would devour us all.

Eventually I fell asleep in the living room. Like a coil, again.

In the morning she walked over to me, sat down beside me on the sofa, and said, "I know you and the things that trouble you. You are a compassionate person and you care for the world. I have never met a man who cares for the world so much and hears people out. I know your grandfather and Mrs. Meeropol have given you a lot of food for thought. They inspire you. And I know what Nat means to you, too, and it all makes you a special person. You know, there is a difference between chatting, flirting, hobnobbing, Facebooking, shopping for vegetables, holding hands, and even getting emotionally involved with someone and then meeting a very special guy like you. I care a lot for you. Don't leave me."

She then got up and went to the bathroom.

CHAPTER NINETEEN

Salvage

There were three of us waiting in the room when she sailed in with yet another manager in tow. A doughy princess figure, she exuded an angry, front-grill arrogance, like she could not wait to run over, bite, maul, and flatten anyone who may appear on her radar. An antithesis to whatever that could be angelic or majestic. I could not help but imagine the worst about her. I imagined the worst, to amuse myself. A bleeding chancre sore in the mouth of a grotesque creature or an anaemic doctor, in a white lab coat, who wore tinted glasses and carried out research on psychotic drugs in a cellar. Or the rusting hull of a condemned trawler in a ship-breaking yard. It all appeared to me in one big rush, like a wave of revulsion that had somehow stayed dormant these past few months since I had set my coordinates on her. Her sun shades were on and her white suit only accentuated her malevolent Nazi-doctor image. A searing headache developed and I saw a thousand images of her, fleeting by and in some of them I saw Nat staring at her, ready to pounce. Ten feet away from me, she stood there—the woman who had come several years ago with the flower-bomb in her hands, and made me an accomplice.

I half expected her to walk in, but I had also considered it unlikely. She was in charge of HR, why would she get involved with Logistics? I watched her closely. She wore the white suit like a lab coat, a silk shirt and a string of pearls around her neck. The hair on the back of my neck must have stood up because I felt cold air sweep down. She spoke with practiced authority, appeared younger than I would have thought. Her manager was a dimwit who nodded at her every statement. It was he who had noticed my background and suggested I head up a team to streamline logistic expenses. Had he shared my resumé with her? Would she not remember that I had worked at the same courier depot where she had dropped off the *dried flowers*? Had she come to check me out?

Every time I looked away from her I sensed she was turning to watch me, and when I tried to return her gaze, her eyes shifted away. It happened a few times. Surprisingly, I didn't feel tense, only disgusted. I was just going to lean back and take it all in slowly.

Here was the project: too many carriers and brokers were registered on the supplier database. It was time to consolidate. She wanted a survey done of shipments into each territory during the last several years broken down into price-per-unit weight. She wanted a thorough job presented on a spreadsheet. The company had the odd practice of making direct shipments to certain customers, even though there were exclusive distributors assigned for various territories. I had already noticed this. It didn't make sense. I was ready to bring it up but she mentioned it.

"As a company, we've had conflicting policies. There are large customers who buy directly from us at a better discount than what we give our distributors, due to past arrangements." Her diction was clear, but I couldn't remember that voice when she came to drop off her package. She continued, "It will not be easy to overcome these legacy issues. Most stem from individual deals made long ago when we didn't have such an elaborate network of distributors. Also, in certain cases, these large companies have a lot of clout and prefer to deal directly, making large bulk purchases under frame agreements. However, it would be worthwhile to note whether or not they are also ordering small quantities at other times. That would inflate our transportation costs unnecessarily."

It sounded like she had already done most of the homework but was inviting a more detailed analysis. The manager, who had a Muppet-like countenance and was appropriately named Bert, immediately piped in. He started up a silly PowerPoint presentation in which a map of the world dissolved into a list of all the distributors in each part of the world. Africa had few distributors—most of the diamonds were coming from there, supplemented with only modest stock from Canada after all—but there was a flood of distributors in the U.S. and Canada, eastern Asia, Europe, and South America. The next slide was only the North American continent, with a range of statistics on the average number of courier drops per month in each geographical district.

She leaned her arms on the glass-topped table as Manager Bert continued to bore us with his presentation. Every now and then she scribbled a few notes on a loose piece of paper. I saw her occasionally looking at me as I, too, took some notes. It was obvious that Bert's numbers were summary and didn't give any immediate clue as to how to meet the consolidation requirements.

The meeting was shortly over. Manager Bert actually seemed surprised as he ran out of slides. Then he announced that I would be required to harvest the database and fill in the details. He wanted to know the weights that were being transported and at what cost and at what frequency. In fact, he directly repeated what Corinthe had already stated. She yawned visibly and stood up, dipped her head a bit to everyone and left, the clicking of her heels fading into the distance.

I, too, rose. I noticed that she had left the scribbled sheets on the desk. I gathered them and pretended to put them in the wastebasket, but actually slipped them quickly into my pocket. She had just fucked up. I had achieved one of my goals on the first day of our encounter! Sweet Jesus! I was locked and loaded! Gerry Banks had specifically told me, "The first thing you do, young man, is to sneak out a recent handwriting specimen from her."

Bert was muttering to himself as he shut down the projector and picked up his laptop. He announced another meeting would be held later and that he'd email all of us further guidelines. I was last out the door. As I closed it I noticed a green glass dome in the ceiling next to the sprinkler; within the dome I saw a lens rotating noiselessly.

I set to work in earnest. The logistical problems were embedded in the way the company had made exceptions along the way. Every rule had at least one exception, some had many more. This had all been exacerbated by the enormous list of suppliers the company was using. Each had different abilities, inabilities, and geographical range of operations. The net impact was that the dispatchers had too many choices: only specific and insider knowledge would allow one to choose the perfect fit for a particular assignment. Too often unexpected complications upset the customers who, of course, didn't understand the reason for them.

After a further week of researching and discussion with the team, I told the Muppet that we had worthwhile recommendations and would like to present them to everyone, implying that Corinthe should be present as well. Of course, the Muppet wanted a preliminary review, with which I complied. It was clear to me that what I had analysed and the solution being proposed was so out of the box that he would have a hard time trying to explain it to her. I had done a fair bit of regression analysis, using newer versions of spreadsheet software to predict that—given the current impact of cost variables—in two years' time current practices would result in a further increase of costs to about 150 percent of its present baseline, mostly due to an increase of avoidable infrastructure. This would directly affect the selling price of the tooling products as well as the abrasive diamond dust and paste the company couriered throughout the world.

I was being an analytical bastard, hungry for recognition in a hyena-chew-hyena word. Bert, of course, had little choice but to agree, given that I had stacked the presentation with compelling details of strapping costs, pallet-racking costs, forklift availability issues, warehousing consumables, IT support and telecommunications, as well as printing consumables and administrative support. It was a report designed to impress, and I did it to unashamedly raise my profile.

The presentation was scheduled during lunch and sandwiches were ordered. The suspect walked in, and for the first time I felt terrified. She had forgotten to take off her famous sunglasses and wore a dress very similar to what she had worn years ago. It was meant to be intimidating. She looked straight at me and never looked away. While I tried my infinite best to stay collected, there were moments when my voice dropped. I cleared my throat twice and she even found a moment to push the water jug towards me. I said *Merci!* And continued.

My solution was unexpected, simple, yet extraordinary. We discovered that the Empire was using nearly sixty different companies for local, airborne, truck, marine, overseas, continental, and national couriering. A new company had come up recently in Montreal called Fourth Party. Originally an Australian company that had specialized in consolidating all the requirements for couriering, including diverse types of packaging, transportation, and shipping, they would be a one-stop solution for everything. They would come to take the product away, package it themselves, warehouse it if necessary, and electronically handle all drop shipments, absorbing the costs that were encountered in personnel, tracking, administration, and delivery. In fact, the last operation in a manufacturing operations sheet would be to "call Fourth Party." They would take charge of the product right on the factory floor at final inspection. Their costs were lower than the lowest we had obtained so far by an average of 10 percent, but more importantly, the internal infrastructure would no longer be necessary. At least twenty workstations could be dropped.

During our team's investigations, we discovered that at least ten times during any month courier companies would come and either wait long hours or get fed up and leave. This was often due to a palette that couldn't be moved the last hundred feet owing to the non-availability of busy forklifts. Fourth Party would come with their own forklifts and their own laptops that interfaced with the company's Enterprise Planning System. They would also initiate a follow-up software that automatically latched on to progress reports by Radio Frequency and GPS devices to provide automatic updates at the planner's desk. In other words, to make it simple, sixty different companies could be replaced by one. They had already made several frame agreements with smaller companies. Our suggestion was a no-brainer. She stared at me again for a while, and then suddenly said, "Looks like you know a lot about couriering." Then the meeting was adjourned. As I was just about to leave the room, she asked me to follow her.

I walked behind her down the long corridor. She invited me into her office for coffee and closed the door behind us. She sat down on the edge of her brown leather-topped, exquisitely ornate and immaculate desk and asked me to sit down. Her legs were crossed, and I think I saw a trace of a smile on her enormously luscious lips. That fucker chiro Roberge must have been biting and sucking them while she folded her tongue and swept the insides of his mouth like a cobra in heat.

"I noticed you worked at the Deltafly courier company on the Main." She had me down. Was she going to frisk me to see if I was wired? "How long were you there?"

"Nearly ten years. Great company. Less complicated work, of course!" I felt composed and unintimidated.

"I think I've been there a few times, but I don't remember seeing you." She was pushing buttons!

"I don't remember seeing you either, but then I was handling over eight to ten customers per hour, and it would also depend on when you came. I often worked at night. When were you last there?" No tremor or hesitation in my voice as I openly lied about the night shift. She did not respond to my question. She slid off the table and went to a corner of the room and poured herself a cup of tea and then came around to her chair and sat down. She didn't offer me anything, even though initially she had asked that I join her for some coffee.

"Did you by any chance pick up some notes I left behind in our first meeting? I think I left them on the desk." Oh, hell! She really did have me. Of course, the green dome on the ceiling. "I went back to look for them and they weren't there."

"Maybe Bert picked them up?" I offered.

She just ignored my answer. "Look, you did a good job and the outsourcing idea is great. Unfortunately, I don't think it will work. Many of the suppliers you want to sideline were actually financed at one time by my father and they'd be upset to be shunted aside. I also know my dad is not going to like it. They will talk to him for sure. But I like the work you did. I'm going to talk to him and see if we can make a compromise. This was a good suggestion, so thanks."

She had her arms folded and wasn't about to shake my hand. I thanked her in return, got up quickly and left the room. Bert, the goof, was waiting outside. I turned around and took one more look. Her arms were still crossed, but she had lowered her head.

That same evening, my old boss from the courier company called to say that an HR firm had called "for references." It was, I thought, a bit late in the process, but I didn't say anything. She had told them I was a great guy, always on my feet, on top of details and a good team worker. I thanked her for her kind support. "You know, Chuck, *mon ami*," she had said at the end, "you can come back any time." I told her it wouldn't be necessary.

The work kept me busy. A week went by with my independent research on the back burner. But then, on the Wednesday afternoon, I was walking down the long corridor and saw her coming towards me. She looked straight ahead and passed by before I could open my mouth to greet her. It was as if I didn't exist.

That evening I went to Myra's apartment to bring her up to date. "Today she walked right by me. I wasn't even worth a glance."

"She's just acting like the rich bitch she is, you know!" Myra didn't hesitate to share her opinion of the suspect, as we referred to her.

"Do you think she's guessed something?" I asked. "I have her writing in my pocket, but I know there was a camera in the room."

"No, she doesn't know. Don't worry, Chuck, you're doing great! She had the case in a freezer for twelve years and now you've got the corpse gently thawing! Hang in there!" Dismal as the thought was, I felt it was logical.

That Thursday morning, I was given the pink slip, no explanation provided. The manager merely said that due to necessary cost cutting they were letting go of a number of people. They didn't have to point out that I had no seniority. I was asked to pack my desk and leave immediately.

And then happened the bone crunch. I was sent flying down the fire escape. The lights went out for nearly three months. The monocular sightline allowed for focus and determination. The periphery was occluded. It was then that I realized we are a composite of so many memories, skills, capabilities, characteristics, nuanced personalities, and distractions. We are a motley mix of fear, courage, strength, and weakness. We are a crowd within ourselves. Our attention span is like that of belly-gazing gnats. Suddenly, we can see better. Night vision, 20/20. Little phosphorescent creatures worm their way out and the red-circled culprit is all that one has to focus on.

When a flood rampages down the rapids, when the snow melts, when that sluice gate in the dam is gently opened, the bottled inertia charges out. I knew what I had to do.

CHAPTER TWENTY

Documentarian Dies

We started at the Commodore and met up with Leo. The restaurant owner recognized the sketch right away and told them that Lipless was one of "them." He didn't want to get too involved and backed away from giving the name, although both Myra and Gerry were convinced he knew. "Sometime," Leo said slowly, "you must stop at the limit. Keep the mouth shut. But the guy is around. He came here a few times with Boswell, who the Gabriella woman know well. Why you want to know?"

Gerry came up with a suitably bland lie. "My son played soccer with him. He had an accident and is now on welfare. He said this guy owes him a lot of money for buying a car, and he can't find him anywhere." It was pretty cool how Gerry could lie on the spot. I understood Myra came by it honestly.

"These guys are bad news," Leo warned. "They hang out on Rachel in the German pub. Stuttgart, I think. You can find him there. But be careful."

By the end of the third month my mobility had increased dramatically, but so had my anger. The police had formally registered the case as a break and enter followed by egregious assault. Having finally defined the crime, they pretty much considered the case shut. Apparently cold cases are in vogue, or at least are often the preferred stalemate.

My home insurance paid for the Tissot watch I had lost, $500 in cash, and another $2,600 in property damage, all based on the thoughtful advice and personal audit by Mr. Banks. There was no police record of any suicide attempt, nor any connection made to my short-lived employment and subsequent dismissal at Gabriel-Jacops Enterprise, Inc.

Now, here is what happens when you finally recover from a serious head, face, and ribcage banging: you realize you are no longer the same person. Life is uncontrollably transformed and undergoes a catalytic conversion. A distance is ensured with those others who you have greeted twice a day or night every day for a decade. Those moments of slouching listless in low couches in eventless neighbourhoods, where nothing can be shared with casual acquaintances whose lives are spectacularly useless—all this comes to a dithering finale. Those pubs and restaurants, frequently visited, where butylated hydroxytoluene replaces buffered aspirin as solace, where intrepid fingers draped in transparent gloves mask the ineptitude of amateur fusion chefs to provide a clear-cut savoury flavour, where cooks boil or poach eggs on pasta and give it an Eritrean alias—that life is no longer of consequence. Those immaculate Saturday afternoons staring through finger-stained window panes, sipping coffee slowly, chewing day-old orange-peel-inserted muffins or unduly hard biscotti while reading unproductively—they, too, somehow fade in importance. They are over. You've been hit square on the jaw and the clock has started to tick and you better do something before they deliver the fatal blow. There is a choice: either go into hiding, seek another identity, and tuck yourself away like an invisible tortoise under a sunless rock; or plan a series of well-considered events, knocking off a merciless To Do list, one by one, while organizing life around the firm decision to win. In other words, my nerd life was over.

"It's time to stick it to them," said Myra, understanding my point. For her, too, it had become personal.

I agreed. I knew my days as a documentarian were over. I could not die as a madman. A suffering documentarian, who would follow a story, then lie down and die in ignominy. Gogol was transformative.

Within a few weeks of my jaw-aching epiphany, the following incident was widely reported in the Montreal police tabloids.

A man with a twisted-and-tucked lip had barely stepped out of the moonlit back door of the tavern on the corner of Rachel when he was approached squarely by a cop with a strange and uncouth beard. He showed him a police badge and in the helium alley light, it could have been a kid's tin cop badge or a flat knuckle-duster in a leather holder. The young man, who reportedly had serious connections with the Montreal underworld, was told, "Just don't say a word. Shut up and cooperate. Okay?" The fellow looked to the side and realized another older cop was positioned behind him. "What the fuck!" is all he could say before a sack—at least that's what it seemed like, but in reality, it was an 817-brand basmati rice jute bag—was slipped over his head and a voice from behind in a distinctly guttural accent said "Say goot bye, now, you useless prig! Your days are numbered. Yes!" He meant to say prick, but it sounded like prig, which made the young thug feel mildly honourable and righteous.

Both cops wore long trench coats and, in some ways, did not seem to be in the greatest shape. The lamplight and the darkness of the alley made this entire operation, carried out at 2 a.m. on a Friday morning, somewhat bizarre. And, as we go along, we shall see that it became increasingly absurd and noteworthy. They handcuffed him, taped his mouth shut, put the basmati rice jute bag over his head, and bundled him into an unmarked van. The driver, according to the man's later testimony, was a policewoman who chewed gum incessantly and noisily. Like "slap-chack-slap-chack-slap" sound and she would look in the rear view and say, "Shut the fuck up or I'll blow yer dickhood away!" Slap-chack-slap-chack. The two men informed him they worked for the "Central Montreal Anti-Gang Squad" and flashed their badges intermittently. As stated earlier, one of the cops had an unknown accent, neither French nor English, and both wore nylons on their faces, facts which provided both confusion and grist for the tabloids. Could it be that this new and secret Montreal police tactical program had adopted a shadowy gangster visage in light of the repeated embarrassment they had faced while dealing with student protestors, who had exposed their identities all too easily?

Two days after being picked up, the near-delirious young thug had surrendered to the police after being abandoned, still handcuffed and with the bag on his head, in front of the Snowdon police station, near Décarie Boulevard. A journalist for the local weekly had been given all the details by an anonymous caller. The police, of course, vehemently denied any such squad, or that this was their operation, and claimed to be totally flummoxed. The gangster, however, was so terrified by the incident that he had confessed to a number of gang-style slayings and violent robberies on camera. He stated that during captivity he had made a videotaped confession about a recent break-in and attempted hit commissioned by a well-known Montreal business tycoon. When released, he stated, the tape would result in a contract on his life, so he wanted protection from the Crown and was willing to do anything to get it. The thug's name was revealed as "Mathieu."

In the months following that event, I enjoyed one of the best periods of my life. I listened to three-piece bands at various bars and lounges all over Quebec in the company of Gerry Banks, Myra, RK, and my grandmother. Gerry was a jazz fiend and followed the scene with radar scanners. He had a list of shows we had to catch taped to his dashboard, and we'd pile into his vehicle and head to remote bars in Quebec City, Knowlton, Gatineau Park, Alma, Mont Tremblant, and sometimes as far away as Chicoutimi and Jonquière. There was something very *family* about all this. We had picnics, we stayed in spas, and we took over lonesome bars in remote locations. I recovered very well, so much so that Nat's absence was a distant thunder roll in the skies, one could say. The music ranged from covers of Thelonius (Blue Monk and Round Midnight), Nat King Cole, Sinatra, and Wes Montgomery, as well as stuff from Cole Porter and Kurt Weill. All this was noted down carefully along the margins of my diary. Yes, noted, but not only.

Icy, snowbound Quebec with towering pine trees and the frozen stillness of brooks in February lay sprawling outside, while inside we enjoyed the keyboard influences of Oliver Jones and Oscar Peterson. Their fond imitators tickled the ivory while we sat around wood fireplaces, ate Quebec lamb, and drank Australian Shiraz—or gulped down Jameson with ice on the side, RK's favourite. His brogues—why had I never noticed this before?—had steel toes. Yes, he wore a trench coat and a fedora tilted belligerently. Some malice there.

Sometimes we sat outside in a hot tub, all five of us in the middle of a snowbound, deeply forested area. My grand-mother, who had never worn a swimsuit before, snuggled up next to RK.

Myra, who was now consistently Myra and not Malia, had transformed into a devastatingly attractive commander of the posse. She was our leader as we stayed in inns, B&Bs, and ski chalets, listening to the music, drinking up a storm, and returning to Montreal planning our ultimate exculpation in the Trois-Pistoles Cold Case. I knew they did it for me.

There were, of course, unexpected complications. There were new procedures to follow, obstacles to overcome. But there was also a concerted and unflagging determination to connect the dots, to get at the full picture of what RK defined, if my memory is correct, as "the dirty, bloody, nefarious, murderous, cynical shenanigans of the rich and the powerful." He'd light up a cigar, narrow his eyes, and a smile would spread at a crooked angle. Detailed planning mattered in such situations and I had a natural skill to go about it well.

RK died in his sleep, six months to the date after this unsolved incident involving the thug Mathieu was widely reported in the Montreal newspapers, leaving many questions unanswered. I had now been deprived of two comrades.

CHAPTER TWENTY-ONE

The Sound of the Scythe

The urn with RK's ashes sits on top of a desk in shrink-wrap held by rubber bands. Years ago, in Montreal, RK had introduced me to Gary at a dim sum place on a Sunday morning on de la Gauchetière. Gary was Chinese but had grown up in Calcutta. He worked at the corner of Rachel and St-Laurent in a designer clothes store. When I told him I was going to Calcutta, he gave me the address of the bed and breakfast. Before I left, he told me, "When you wake up in the morning, it will still be dark and you will hear the sound of crows congregating on the rooftop railing of the house next door. Listen carefully and you will hear the sound of a scythe slicing the moist grass on the rooftop of that house. You will see a man with blue eyes and a sharp nose. He is my dad. Say hello to him."

The floor-to-ceiling curtain in my room is motionless. Through a part in the fabric, I can see silhouettes moving in the dark outside. The silhouettes cannot see me. There is a lawn approximately twelve feet by fifteen feet on top of the fifth-floor roof of the house next door. I can see the black wrought-iron railings about two feet high around the perimeter of the lawn. The green of the grass is in my mind only. I remember it from the day before. Yesterday morning I had checked into this bed and breakfast in Calcutta.

As the first rays of the sun penetrated through the dusty sky, bluish black crows appeared from somewhere and were assembling on the railing in the near darkness. One by one their silhouetted wings settle as they gather, as if they have been called to a conference. One by one they move sideways as if taking designated spots. A glow appears in the sky towards the east of the city, where the railroad line leads. The night has been impatient and ready to depart. One can hear the squealing on rails of multiple diesel engines slowly pulling an endless line of wagons carrying oil, copper wire, steel cable, and wheat at a remote distance. With the growing light the crows become more prominent. They are surprisingly quiet. Or are they being congenial, as if in a subdued and conversational mode? I expect that as the day progresses they will become ever more querulous.

There must be a lone sweeper sweeping the narrow street with a long broom. I can hear the broom as it occasionally hits patches of water from the rain that fell last night. The crows look down upon him and nod their heads as they continue to occasionally shuffle sideways. There is nothing else to be heard. There is absolute stillness everywhere.

I am lying on my bed and know that in the adjacent houses they are hearing the same sounds. I know everyone in this B&B is probably horizontal like me, but I am wide awake and only I can see through this crack in the curtain towards my own private revelation, my own special invitation to acknowledge the teasing day and the release of night. I can't yet smell anything. Calcutta has still not released its odours. I can see, I can hear, but I can't smell.

The rays of the sun split open the clouds of night. The spiral stair from the fourth-floor roof curving up to this plot of green is now clearly visible, its wrought-iron filigree reminding me of a twirling flamenco dancer. In the quiet of my head the heraldic horn of Miles Davis accompanies the filigree—the Concierto de Aranjuez? The plaintive, distant trumpet releases a series of single notes. I continue to lie on my stomach and stare through the crack. No one in the neighbourhood can see any of this except me because it is only this B&B that overlooks it. There are no other buildings high enough to see this lawn with the spiral staircase. Then I hear the sound of the scythe slicing the air.

The name of the Chinese-American-Indian gardener is Feng. No one goes up there except him. He has dark, tawny skin and his eyes are blue. The owner of the building lives three floors below. He used to design silk scarves and made a fortune doing so. Today he doesn't climb those stairs. The Chinese-American-Indian man does, because it's his job to maintain an impeccable lawn in the city fifty feet above ground. And no one else at this moment is experiencing this garden except me.

On the fourth-floor rooftop terrace there are kiss-me-quicks, bougainvillea vines, chrysanthemums, rose bushes, and varied shades of green shrubbery in terracotta containers, all neatly trimmed and arranged like a horticultural para-dise. There is a wrought-iron railing around that terrace, too. There is a woman who comes up every morning around ten to the fourth-floor garden to hang clothes and curtains, to wash cloths and towels that have never seen the inside of a dryer. She curves her body around the bonsai trees that grow in rectangular ceramic pots to hang everything on a large, stainless steel rack. Her blouse stretches over her body and exposes a large expanse of sculpted midriff. The sun is now firmly positioned above the horizon.

Feng carefully trims the lawn on the fifth floor and it looks like a rice field from my large sliding windows. Beads of sweat appear on his forehead. He raises his little sickle to greet her. She brings him a glass of water. He squats on the grass and asks her to leave it at the bottom of the spiral stairs. His thirst must wait until he has finished trimming the grass uniformly like a carpet. I wonder if she has ever seen the fourth-floor lawn. He works soundlessly like a Taekwondo warrior. His every move is coordinated, a soundless and continuous act of stealth and beauty. His calf muscles are the first to constrict and then stretch as they transfer their energy through the rest of his body like a quiet wave that passes through his torso and then the arm to end in the hand holding the handle of his sickle.

Feng was born in Nanking to a Chinese woman and an American official. That was before the Second World War. The Kuomintang of Chiang Kai Shek had come to power around 1927 after he split from the Communists. Criminal gangs were let loose on the streets of Nanking to scalp Communists and other Nationalist factions. Foreigners scurried away. The American official had been sent in as an advisor to the Kuomintang. In all probability, he was a second-rate espionage agent who spent less time officiating than he did socializing. Young Feng was left behind in an orphanage and adopted by a British woman, named Sara Hopkinson, who moved around Southeast Asia during the Second World War collecting jade statues. Young Feng went from country to country with his adoptive parent. Eventually they settled down in Calcutta, India. Sometime after India gained independence Ms. Hopkinson decided to sell the antique store she owned on Park Street, Calcutta. She left for London, but Feng stayed behind.

At the age of eighteen, Feng had been well employed driving a truck for the U.S. Army at Fort William. That was in the early forties, or maybe a bit later. The Americans were bored and had nothing to do other than go to the Red Cross

Society and play cards or walk around in the Hogg Market Area bargaining for Gurkha *bhojali* knives from Nepalese hawkers. When Feng's adoptive mother went to the Fort William Club on Saturday evenings, Feng would go with her. It was there that he met a Jewish officer from New Jersey named Berger, who hired Feng. The truck was the common mode of conveyance for the GIs and Feng knew his way around the city. While his Chinese features were vaguely discernible, his American ancestry was clear through his blue eyes and sharp nose.

From the crack between the curtains as the sun came up, I saw Feng squatting on the green lawn while a Star of David flopped on his chest. Mr. Berger had given it to Feng when he went back to the United States. Feng married an Indian woman, Radha, in the early fifties, and they had two children.

I did say hello to Feng and we became friends. He spoke in short sentences and lifted his chin to make a point. One day, in the early afternoon, I asked him to have lunch with me. I sat with him at a Punjabi restaurant on the main road in Gariahat, Calcutta, and he told me his story between sips of chai and pieces of pakora.

"My boss make silk scarves. He hired me as his driver. Big business. I take him everywhere. When my eyes go bad, he say that I become a gardener and stay in his building. I say okay." He said this and then raised his chin, making sure it was clear.

"And your wife? Radha?" I asked with hesitation.

"Oh, she leave me. She take my daughter with her. I don't know where they are."

He wiped the sweat from his forehead and looked out the window. A garishly coloured tramcar, with dents and scratches, rattled by with folks holding onto it precariously. "But Gary is in Canada. He send money every few months. He good boy. He do some college. And then he leave for Canada. He say I must come. I say what for? I am happy; I cut the grass, best lawn in Calcutta on the rooftop."

He smiled and I saw that he had gold fillings on his side teeth. "How come the grass is so green?" I asked with genuine interest.

"Chlorophyll," he pronounced it very clearly and stopped, his blue eyes waiting for me to understand.

"Yes, I know grass has chlorophyll which absorbs blue and red light and bounces back green light, but what do you do to make the grass have so much chlorophyll?" I wanted him to speak to me. I wanted to tell Gary something insightful about his father and what he did. But mostly, I thought about RK and the connections he had that slowly unravelled on this trip.

He said, "Oh! Nothing! Just put down some cow dung . . . aged. And lots of water . . . in the evening mainly. Yes." He smiled a little.

"What do you want me to tell Gary?" I asked after a long silence.

"The grass is green! He can come and see it sometime, maybe?" His watery blue eyes stared at the street behind us. An arrow had burrowed its way through my chest and exited soundlessly past my vertebral column only to flop down on the Main. Another rickety tramcar roared by with passengers clinging to it.

Gary had given me some light cotton shirts to give to his father and also a panama hat and a large jar of multivitamins. Feng examined everything very carefully and said, "Say thank you to him."

On my last day in Calcutta, Feng had two packages for me. He told me they were a special gift for Gary. He opened the first and showed me a blade of grass that he had had plasticized and mounted on a piece of sky blue cardboard with clouds painted on it, around which he had glued small strands of gold and red silk as if they were flying through the sky. The whole thing had then been framed in glass.

He didn't open the second package. He simply told me to give it to Gary. He bowed to me gently and stepped back. I bowed to him. I looked up at the wrought-iron rails for one last time and left for the airport. In the plane, my thoughts criss-crossed the cumulous clouds.

I had lived a life between RK and Nat. RK was always an insider. He read, studied, thought, and remarked. He gave direction. Nat lived on the outside. He sensed, but did not discuss much. Now, although I missed all that, I was also past that. Here I was following a trail set by RK and Nat. Taking a break from what was to follow. Everything they had done or said triggered connected emotions. Egged you on. The crowd in you manifested in so many ways. The pasting of Mathieu was just the start to the tangle with the headquarters. Now followed the sojourn to find the friend who had left the playing fields, because those fields did not fit him well any longer.

CHAPTER TWENTY-TWO

Nomad

I trundled off the mini-bus somewhere just north of Arghandab district, northwest of Kandahar City. My backpack, though light, was unwieldy. I was not carrying many items in it and those I had kept shifting.

Heavy vehicles swerved and careened along unpaved roadways. Helicopters thundered above, chopping the air and disappearing over hills towards mountains. The dull thump of occasional mortars resonated in the distance. My sojourn had begun, a hard journey following more than a year of recuperation. I was on an uncertain path after my abrupt departure from the fragile faces that were sad to see me leave.

A strange feeling, walking on a road covered with flying debris, red dust, and reddish-brown pebbles, not along the carefully sculpted, brass-plate-inserted, block-by-block address-providing, cemented, pristine sidewalks I was used to. As the ground below my feet rumbled, I gazed up. The sky in Afghanistan wasn't the same, either: it was spectacularly clear above me.

I had come to spread his ashes. And I had come to meet him.

I continued forward, bewildered by the glare of the sun and thinking about the more recent jottings in my diary.

"When would I again hear the sound of Myra's clicking heels on the pavement along the Main as she strode towards me in her large sunglasses? Would I ever? Would I smell again her warm sweaty fragrance, a combination of some pleasant hormonal release and the gentle trace of last night's perfume? Would I ever grab her and lift her high?"

My legs wobbled. My limbs felt both uninhibited and uninhabited, with neither discipline nor vigour. The repairs done to my shins had given them a life of their own. Sometimes my right leg kicked out without having asked permission to do so. I felt a systemic decay throughout my body: in my toes, between them, behind my ears, in my groin, in my knees. My face still felt partially entombed, the skin of my jaw raw and stretched as if nylon threads held it together.

Myra used to wash my chest, back, and arms with warm water and isopropyl alcohol to provide temporary relief. Then she'd put unscented cream around my elbows and heels, which were dry and cracked. She finished with warm socks on my feet, which the nurses appreciated. She had helped recover my body as much as it had been recovered, and had done it slowly and meticulously. I had never known she could be so patient, or so determined.

For months after surgery—with the help of antibiotics, analgesics, and the sub-conscious drifting in and out of disjointed words and phrases that repeated themselves inside my mind—I slowly pulled myself together into a new entity capable of humming tunes that hadn't previously existed.

But while I carried the past with me, I was no longer the same person. In the middle of the night I'd wake up to hear the sounds of a bewildering set of people about my bed. Their hazy forms floated, mumbled, whispered to each other: words of concern, of despair, of warning. I distinctly remember being visited by two dark shadows in the room ready to strike me and kick me when down; I saw again the glow in the doorway behind Mrs. Meeropol as I lay down on her living room sofa; I suffered the grimaces of the gargoyles on the rooftops of Boulevard St-Laurent as icy water dripped from their nostrils; I again saw the freeze frame of Nat leaning against a lamppost, cigarette hanging loose from the side of his mouth, a few days after his dad passed away. I was again visited by Myra entering the café with the runs in her stockings spreading geographically, furiously chewing gum, reporting on recent sightings with the energy of a leaping impala. Then she transformed into the brooding Malia, the dark dancer with lips on fire who wrapped herself around me.

Before RK departed he had written a note for me. He suggested, very politely, that I visit Calcutta, now renamed Kolkata, and take a walk along the Strand beside the River Hooghly. I'd eventually reach the man-o-war jetty, where I'd most probably find a boat at anchor. I should ask the boatmen to take me some distance into the river and then quietly release his ashes into the river when no one was watching.

So I had to go, not for my father, but to be with RK in his own world. It was not a religious ritual, just an appropriate return waiting to be accomplished.

I had slowly opened the lid of the ceramic urn and emptied the ashes into the Hooghly, the boatman urging me to lean far over so the ashes wouldn't drift back towards me. I did so. I watched as the remains of a PhD candidate from Montreal found their way into a muscular swirl of the muddied Hooghly and then drifted away in a twisting torrent of palm twigs and tears. Looking to the distance I saw the foggy outline of the majestic second Hooghly Bridge claw the sky.

After I finished in India, I took a plane from New Delhi to Kabul and then on to Kandahar by bus. That bus trip was advised by a well-meaning idiot in Delhi who had thought it would be more pleasant than another flight. So, when the extremely well-mannered and kind bus driver swerved precariously around one poorly repaired bomb crater only to descend into another, this happening all along the 482-kilometre stretch, my eyes closed in agony as my tibia rose to butt against my patella while the meniscal cartilages desperately tried to shoulder the responsibility of the bus's missing shock absorbers. I yelled whatever came naturally. My frequent *tabernacs*, however, had no effect, falling as they did on deaf ears.

At Qarah Bach, halfway through, I got off the bus and lay down on the ground in absolute agony. I even lifted my jeans to show the bus driver the deep scars on my knees and ankles. I also pointed out the lateral gashes that swept around my shin bones where the fire escape steps had interrupted the descent. The kind bus driver nodded, convinced I had lived the experience of being blown up by an IED. I tried to make him understand that there were no IEDs happening in Canada, not as yet, and that I had fallen down some stairs and was saved by snow. He smiled compassionately and said "Oh! Ya! Snow! Good! Good!"

Perhaps he believed in my story, perhaps he was convinced I was a lunatic, in any case after we climbed back on the bus he cleared a space between the two wheel wells and arranged for me to sit there. A Dutch reporter who had earlier grabbed the spot felt he was being unfairly treated and went to the back complaining.

I again looked up. There were no birds in the sky, just the icy trails of fighter jets criss-crossing in the northern sky. The hills were bare and rocky. The dull thumps could still be heard. Who would spot me? How would they know who I was looking for? Why would they bother to meet me?

Nat had been incommunicado for months and Mrs. Meeropol had slowly shrunk into a tentative old lady.

Ava's glow was gone. I found it difficult to look at her as she gazed at me with her head tilted to the side, asking in silence an unanswerable question. When she finally received an email with the recent details of his whereabouts she almost broke down. He had told her that he was no longer working for the company that had hired him to run security operations for Canadian NGOs.

"Then why is he still there?" she exclaimed, pleading. "What is he doing there? Why isn't he coming back?"

I decided then to tell Mrs. Meeropol that I was going to Calcutta to deliver RK's ashes and would return via Afghanistan. She had looked up, smiled, and hugged me lightly. She clearly thought that was the right thing to do. She looked into my eyes and once again I realized that there is something about her and people like her that profoundly moves me. They don't have their noses to the ground sniffing for opportunities; rather, like RK, they breathe the air for fresh scents of hope. She and RK were similar in this way, they not only remembered, they respected.

I didn't bother to tell her that Kandahar was far from Kolkata, that between India and Afghanistan lay Pakistan, that between the Ganges and the Amu Darya and the Arghandab rivers lay ranges, deserts, plains, mountains, caves, towns, villages, sandstorms, hostile tribals, insane fanatics, and reckless invading soldiers. Kandahar was not a simple ride away. But I was deeply involved in her and her son's lives, and no matter what, he was my buddy.

I sent a return message giving him my date of arrival and asking where to meet. He eventually sent back one very short sentence. I was to find the bus station, not wander far, have tea if I wanted, and wait.

Simple.

CHAPTER TWENTY-THREE

Ten Paces Ahead

It wasn't easy to wait calmly. No one but the merchants stood around long. Everyone else kept moving. Heads covered by shawls. The tension was palpable, with the repeated IED blasts that happened in the area.

I was wearing a worn pair of jeans, a dark shirt that hung low over them, an old imitation DKNY jacket and a brown shawl around my neck like a scarf. As I looked up I saw columns of buildings, sometimes three stories high that had been sliced down like a multi-layered cake, nothing remaining except sheer walls with exposed bricks and the remnants of door frames and windows. There were piles of bricks around the feet of these sheared buildings. There were walls around some of them, but they, too, were in various stages of collapse. It didn't reassure me that American soldiers assigned to Company A, 1st Battalion, 4th Infantry Regiment, wearing full regalia—sand camouflage uniforms, robot headgear, chest plates, radio mikes, and dark shades—walked around single file pointing their outsized assault guns at everyone's knees.

A man was selling green and yellow vegetables, which, from the distance, I took to be squash. Beside him stood another man wearing a brick-coloured caftan with a black jerkin over it and a dark brown turban on his head. He looked from side to side, but never at me. Behind him a white mini-van had sunk into the ground, tire-less, bullet riddled, and with all the windows gone. I heard radio chatter coming from an Indian-made Mahindra jeep parked nearby. I also heard an ominous drum being thumped in the distance.

Pashtun men walked by, speaking quietly, their dusty faces barely visible behind their shawls. Where I was standing there were no women in sight. The boys walking with them were quiet and, like the men, wore no socks.

A delegation of Canadian families arrived and gathered under a grey sand tent. I imagined they had come for "final closure," a program introduced by the Canadian government to allow families of killed soldiers to visit the land where their loved ones had perished. It was, I thought, a feeble yet brave exercise, and I wondered if any other nation had undertaken the same. But there are ways in which the death of one's young can be made acceptable, and perhaps this was one of them. I walked to another section of the bus terminal, which seemed sufficiently large to function as a kind of town centre.

It started to drizzle. The rain didn't bother anyone. No one, nor did I, try to take shelter under the many tent-like stalls. There were women visible here, almost all of them in pale blue burqas. I also saw, sitting under a tent awning, two extraordinarily pretty young girls in their teens with brilliant smiles that revealed their gums. They wore chadors on their heads and giggled. There was a dusty tone to their skin and I imagined the enormous mix of ethnicities that might be racing through their veins. Their roots could be Greek, Jewish-Aramaic, Babylonian, Syrian, Persian, Uzbek, Mongol or, of course, Pashtun; just some of the people who had once upon a time set foot in Afghanistan to never leave. In fact the very name of Kandahar was said to be a derivative of Alexander, which in Pashto was pronounced Iskandar. All these races had mingled in this land—some long before the birth of Christ. In fact, the Pashtuns themselves could very well have started out as a mix of Jewish and Persian tribes.

I was looking for Nat, the Canadian, from Montreal. I returned to the tea stall where I had first stood. I finally decided my knees needed the rest and I walked into the tent. I sat on a bench and a young boy immediately handed me a milky mug of tea with buttery froth floating on top. I sipped it carefully and enjoyed it, feeling its thick warmth spread through my body. It tasted like goat's milk.

The few dark eyes peering from the deeper recesses of the tent were staring at me. I looked at the ground with a simultaneous sense of wariness and reflection. Myra drifted by in my mind and I immediately straightened my back and thought of her eyes, the warmth of her hugs, and again heard her voice. Chuck, you won't do anything silly, right? Chuck, if you don't find Nat now there'll be another time. I'm not stopping you, but think of what we have here. It's not finished yet, Chuck, so don't walk away from me. You have to come back, you know that, don't you baby?

Outside the tent an all-terrain vehicle kicked up dust and roared away, crates of oranges visible on the back. Had some local managed to find supplies meant for the GIs and was transporting it home however he could? Who knows the values of the supplies that never made it to their intended destination, whether it be oranges, grapes, or grenades?

When the dust settled, I saw the tall Pashtun man who had been standing next to the squash seller come toward the tea stall. On the other side of the street I saw another tall person standing against the shadow of an isolated pillar. She had a shawl wrapped around her head, covering most of her face. I could only see her very sharp aquiline nose. She watched the first man crossing the street. I held my breath for a few seconds, knowing something was about to happen. He came straight towards me, bent his tall body so he could get into the tent and said "please," pointing outside with an open palm.

I immediately put down my mug of tea, left some money on the wooden table, and followed him. The woman had already started walking and was about fifty paces ahead of us. There was no conversation for the next two hours as I walked quickly behind the two of them. We walked the length of several streets, then emerged behind a grouping of houses, followed several dustier alleyways before passing a soccer field and, finally, walking through an open field with pebbles, rocks, and clumps of underbrush growing at irregular intervals.

I noticed that many buildings I passed had blue mosaic tiles on their dome-like roofs. The colour, apparently, had remained *fashionable* for centuries. I was becoming exhausted and my shins hurt. The man continued ten feet ahead and the tall woman fifty paces ahead of him. I looked to the sky for drones carrying hellfire missiles. I knew they had become the standard operational procedure: several hits per week, all of which—or so it was claimed—only killed terrorists, the worst of the worst, but then a day or two later it inevitably emerged that someone's extended family had been wiped out. This was followed by routine denials, then apologies, and then a reaffirmation the forces would be more careful.

After we had walked through another small village and left it behind too, I saw we were headed straight towards a blue ridged mountain. The sun was setting and the mountain cast a long dark shadow on the ground in front of us. Above, birds flew around in large circular orbits. I was now visibly in pain. My escort slowed down. It was only then that I noticed the woman who had been walking fifty paces ahead had been replaced with another guide who marched with similar vigour. He wore a long Afghan salwar kameez, which was black. He also had a black shawl wrapped around him that covered most of his upper torso. I suddenly felt a wave of apprehension. Only the Taliban wore black.

We reached the crest of a hill where five elderly men sat overlooking a cliff. I noticed that they had not lit a fire, despite the fact it was getting cooler. Thermal cameras hovered in the skies. What a state of siege! The coming darkness and cold made me shiver. Plumes of smoke rose from a peak high to the north, twisting like Pashtun headgear in the skies. The large, billowing, genii-like, ayatollah clouds coiled up and hovered over the mountain capturing the colours of the sunset. The man in black pointed toward that direction and talked to the four elders as they looked up at the horizon. One of the elders didn't care to look, his face disdainfully turned away, preferring to stare at the pebble-strewn soil around his feet.

Somewhere in the sky a fighter went supersonic and the Mach cone came down with a series of thunder claps that rattled the entire valley. The man in black had a compact sub-machine gun hanging from his shoulder, which, until now, I hadn't noticed. It had a folding butt stock and a pistol grip, and was a new variant of an AK-56. I had diligently studied weaponry, including improvised explosive devices, as preparation for this trip. I had crawled the web, fearful, cautious, and a bit excited. Wires, detonators, battery packs, Semtex, C-4, packaging, colour codes were all new concerns in my current life.

My guide, who by now I knew as "Ten Paces Ahead," broke the news that we would be spending the night right there. When he said "here," I had the inclination to look around and say "where?" but restrained myself. It was then I noticed a small shed built of bricks and tarpaulin against the side of the cliff.

One of the elderly men looked like Fidel Castro with a high nose and a full beard. He was fair complexioned and his blue eyes were sad and droopy. Another had no moustache, but wore a well-rounded and precisely trimmed beard. He was scratching the top of his head after removing his Afghan hat. They all looked from the sides of their eyes and no one seemed to have any inclination whatsoever to engage me in any discussion.

A thick blanket hung down like a door to the shed, the floor of which was surprisingly well prepared and smooth. Several rolled up blankets had been neatly arranged inside. Ten Paces Ahead, whose real name he told me was Hameed, pulled out an aluminum container from under his shawl. It was a food hamper with bread and roasted meat. No fires were lit. We squatted down on the floor and attacked the food. The man in black stayed outside briefly and then he, too, disappeared, as had the elders. I thanked Hameed for dinner. There was a canteen of water with which I washed my hands.

The sun had finally disappeared and the distant mountain rose like a restless jinn in the dark. The dull thump of explosions continued. I sat outside and looked at the hills. As my eyes adapted to the darkness, I saw sand bags along the edges of the hill-top and beside it an old generator with handle grips lying on its side. I walked over and picked up two shiny 7.62-mm spent cartridges among the many lying about and put them in my pocket.

As I looked across the valley I saw no lights anywhere.

I went back inside and Hameed was reading a book with the help of a Swiss Army flashlight. It seemed everything was well planned and he knew why I was there. There was no reason to ask him the plan. I covered myself with the musty smelling blankets and quickly fell asleep.

It must have been about four in the morning when he woke me. Once again, the man in black stood paces away in the distance. This time we walked down the hill with Hameed using his flashlight to show the way. He aimed the light in such a way that he could see the path and his legs were silhouetted so I could follow. We walked like that for an hour before we came to the outskirts of a small town. I believe it may have been Pir Zadeh or Per Zidah. There was a sign, but I'm pretty sure the writing was in Pashto.

The sun had begun to bob on the horizon when we reached a small enclave of houses. We entered one and I was asked to sit in a room with an open door. The man in black remained outside. Hameed left. He never said good-bye, just disappeared. I put my backpack down and sat on a wooden bench. Once again, a young boy appeared out of nowhere. He gave me an empty mug and flashed me a smile. As I held the mug he poured the strong-smelling tea from a pot that was twice the size of his head. He lifted it up deftly and tilted the curved spout and the milky tea came out in a gush of steam. It cleaned the insides of my mouth and generally felt good going down the throat.

"Taliban key ma key chut! That's it, that's all." *The Taliban's mama's cunt, that's it that's all.* I was in a relaxed state of bewilderment when I overheard this conversation between the guy in black and someone else outside. I had learnt a few choice Urdu words from Indian and Pakistani friends when I was at Concordia University, but I thought this a frightening exchange in a country under the firm grip of the Taliban. Immediately, a Pakistani man wearing salwar kameez and an Afghan hat stepped in. His Guevara beard was a handsome contrast to the long beards or the orange-tinted trimmed ones prevalent in the town centre. He had a shoulder holster with a sub-compact machine gun hanging from it. It was partially covered by his shawl but clearly visible. He stepped in and said "Salaam Walekhom" to me and plunked himself down on the opposite bench. The sun had risen and was funnelling its first rays in long spikes over the Afghan mountains. I greeted him back, "Walekhom Salaam".

He introduced himself as Shaheed and held out his hand. I shook it. "You are looking for your friend. He's with us. He knows you're coming and is looking forward to seeing you. There are certain rules to be followed and both you and I are going to follow them to the letter. Okay? Otherwise the *behnchoot kuttey* drones will send the fireball up our arses and that, I've heard, is unpleasant. You will cover your head with your shawl completely and you will not speak unless you are spoken to. We are going to make a very short trip to the other side of town in the van."

"Sure," I said calmly.

We got into a small van waiting outside. I considered it a perfect target for a drone. It had a noisy diesel engine, no windows and at least five people already packed in, as well as the man in black. I got into a rear passenger seat and dipped my head to the people sitting next to me. Everyone smelt of unpasteurized goat milk. The van roared off and left the little enclave behind in no time. It climbed the side of a mountain and then, after about ten minutes, Shaheed drove it straight into a narrow pass and parked it under a cliff overhang expertly carved out of the side of a rock face, large enough for a number of cars. The men in the back all trooped out and went down a hill. We got out and entered another cliff-top settlement, but this one with signs of family activity. I saw a man playing with a child. There were huts carved into the sides of a hill and I thought I saw women in the distance, their faces exposed but their heads covered. In the middle of the settlement there was a clearing, like a plaza. It was composed of dry, red clay and at the edge of it, standing still, with the rays of the morning sun bouncing off his teeth, was Nat, a huge smile on his face.

He was lankier and had grown a long beard. He was wearing a salwar kameez with a large shawl wrapped loosely around his head and neck. All about were small groups of men, dressed somewhat similarly, with sophisticated weapons slung over their shoulders, a few with rocket launchers on their backs. Shaheed swung over to the other side of the car and said a few things to the man in black before coming around and leading me to Nat.

We stared at each other and I maintained the discipline of not speaking till I was spoken to, when Shaheed in his boisterous style said "So—like man!—this is a Montreal party!" He had quite the character, flamboyant mannerisms married to a refined appreciation for danger.

I said to Nat as gently as I possibly could, "Hey!"

He put his arms around me and we hugged as brothers. "Hey," he finally replied, "I'm known as Azmat around here."

CHAPTER TWENTY-FOUR

It's Over

I felt I had just walked through a dark tunnel at night into a desert, through a hopeless arid valley and an endless descent into a dark hole with hostile elements and then—there was sunshine. And yet, inside me, I already sensed that this was edging toward catastrophe. I imagined an explosion happening at any moment and our bodies flung in a hundred pieces through the air to land in splotches on the sloping valley.

In the dark dress of Azmat with his tanned, tawny skin, Nat stood like one of his Hollywood heroes, Sir Alec Guinness or maybe Peter O'Toole. I was not sure.

I put my arms around him and we went into a hut, Shaheed accompanying us. After tea had been placed in our hands, Nat asked about his mother. I told him all I could. Then I went on to tell him what had happened to me in the last year and a half. "It's been hard, especially the slow recovery while in hiding." He looked at me. "You're grown, man! Don't go back to the hood. It's over."

Suddenly, "What's Myra up to?" Looking at me directly with his penetrating eyes.

"We're thick as thieves! I would have rotted in hell if she hadn't been around." I explained how she had settled down, with Gerry in the picture, and that she was working part-time at a production company while still going to the occasional audition.

Now if he had said, *you've gotta be kidding,* I wouldn't have been surprised, but he simply said, "Yeah," as if, somehow, he already knew. I went on to explain how I had applied for the job with the Enterprise and how nervous I had been.

"You know what I think? I think they knew you were after them the moment you applied. But they wanted to confirm it, so they took you on. You look good, man! Not the same guy. You're kind of changed." Shaheed smiled knowingly.

I was taken aback by his certainty. But I knew as well that I was no longer the same. I *had* changed. He took a deep breath, clenched his fist and punched the palm of his other hand, then looked away in disdain. Sipping tea, he finally opened up and spoke with a subdued rage. "Let me tell you, I know stuff I didn't before. It's all connected. Connected!" He webbed his fingers together. "You know what I mean? I was just hanging out, lazing on the Main. The fuckin' Plateau Mont-Royal! Right? Nothing really bothered me. I just wanted a break in acting. Doing this, doing that. Nothing of significance. I wasn't into any of the serious stuff. My mom was disappointed that I wouldn't talk history with her. I wasn't like you."

"She needs someone to talk to," I said. "You know how it is, she has her feet in two worlds and wants to know how one fits with the other."

"Your grandfather had it right. He changed my thinking. He changed me. I'm really sorry about him." He lowered his head.

The mention of RK cut a blowtorch through me as usual. Nat understood. Tears swelled up in my eyes.

He continued, "RK knew what was going on. It ain't about terrorism or retribution. 9/11 etc. That's all bullshit!

There's a thin layer of moral superiority on top, to hide a thick layer of business and military interests below. We've sanitized our terrorism to make it look good. You know what I mean? Every freakin' day a drone hits a village and kills innocent people. Every day! Little kids blown to bits." I stared into his eyes. He was not the same either. I saw a weathered fighter. His skin was furrowed. The parallel lines on his forehead reminded me of the tram lines that still pop up on Montreal streets, steel rails emerging through old asphalt. Deep trenches had formed beside his mouth and the speckles of sand within them glistened like sparks.

It was weird to hear Nat talk like this, angry. During all our years in Montreal, we had never spoken about these things. We might have joked about them, but never really *spoken* about them. I read stuff and discussed it with RK; but Nat was right, we had both preferred to have a good time gawking and dreaming. That had been good enough. I now knew what he was talking about because I had changed, too. The writer in me had ceased to exist. The guy who wanted to document had died. We had started to live in each other's lives. In the lives of our neighbourhood, our parents and grandparents. Everything had become a composite of everything else that we shared. The characters, the relatives, and the folks we liked or disliked. We had absorbed them all. That is what it was all about.

"Nothing we do here is right, man! We piss on their religion, on their corpses, kill the wrong people in combat and then slay the innocents in psychotic fits and pretend like it never happened."

At this point Shaheed took a loud slurp of the tea and interrupted. "We're not the fucking Taliban in case you're getting worried. The creepy *madarchods*. We are with no one, which is, by itself, a problem, wouldn't you say brother

Azmat?" Saying that, he slapped his knees and then slapped Nat on the back and let out a shrieking laugh.

I smiled, finally beginning to relax.

Nat took the shawl off his head. There were streaks of premature grey in his beard. "I came here with Blue-Sky to protect government installations, including a couple of field hospitals. The company liked me. You know, they were impressed by my martial-arts training, my physical fitness, and I guess they liked my engaging personality." He winked and for a split second the old Nat was back. "In the beginning, I worked on the perimeter defence near the airport, setting up the bollards mainly, to prevent suicide bombers. I designed some of the installation as well as worked on security detail."

"What's a bollard?"

"They're like solid cylinders. They can be permanent upright or designed to retract into the ground. They can take a lateral force of a 15,000-pound vehicle at 50 miles per hour and bring the vehicle to a stop in three feet. Sometimes, when there's no space to use hydraulics, they're physically pulled up from buried canisters and then locked by a bayonet-style pin arrangement. You put a farm of these on the ground and it's a strong deterrent."

I said nothing.

"But then things started to happen and I wanted to leave. You know about the friendly fire incident. Well, some dumbass pilot, very friendly no doubt, dropped two laser-guided 500-pounders on our soldiers. Reckless sonofabitch. They don't give a shit, man! Listen! I can tell you stuff that you're never going to see on Global or on L fuckin' TV."

"How'd you join up with these folks?" I was looking at Shaheed.

"They're different. They saved my ass from a Taliban IED. They pulled me out of a ditch and the device exploded a few seconds later. It was a crimson fireball going up and hot metal pieces coming down. Wherever they fell they burned right through. These guys aren't no whacko fanatics. They're plain nationalists who don't want any of this Taliban sharia shit. Freedom fighters. And they aren't working with any of the warlords, either." Shaheed stood and said, "You two talk. We've a couple of hours left."

Nat wanted to speak. "During one of my security details I realized something screwy was going on. Gruesome. It wasn't clear if our forces themselves were doing the roughing up, because they interrogated in rooms right adjacent to the rooms of the Afghan Security Police. Our military police had handed them over to Intelligence personnel who had come from Ottawa, and they had 96 hours to get whatever information they could. There was always a rush. The rush made them do things that were not right and then they handed them back to the Afghan police who are nothing but fuckin' rogues. Outsourcing the torture. Most of the local soldiers aren't Pashtuns. They're Tajiks mainly and that's a big friggin' problem. We're on one side of an ethnic conflict."

Then I asked him the only important question I had to ask. I knew he was waiting for it. "So are you staying here or going back?"

He hesitated. "Not right now, for sure, man!" He wrung his hands. "What am I gonna do there in Montreal? I'm already too far away from all that! I took a couple of weeks to travel to Greece when I was with Blue-Sky and I was miserable, man. I couldn't sit still. I was so restless I scared myself. My normal has changed. You know what I mean? What am I gonna do sitting in a bistro on Mont–Royal? I'll want to empty a magazine. That's not cool, is it? Who is going to help me when I get back? I dunno. I feel I got one foot on the platform and the other on the train."

My insides knotted. Getting back to "normal" was probably out of the question.

"And I wasn't even in direct combat. Can you imagine the kids from Valcartier and Petawawa? Some of them have never been out of their province and now they're here, in over their heads. You think they can return to normal? There are no programs, you know? Just the chaplains and then flying visits from Ottawa by some PTSD specialists. What good is that? I know I have it! For sure I have it. That's why I'll never get out of here."

He struggled with himself and then concluded, "Actually, this is better. I don't have to deal with the shit in the normal world. Here I live the tension. You hear the thump and in your mind you see the blood gurgle out of a blown-out head. That's normal." And he smiled.

That was not normal. This was not Nat. And then his face changed.

"And I tell ya. The shit in Montreal is all insipid. I'm done with that. I'm done with all the petty tribal warfare. You think these guys are tribes? Hell no! Here the shit is real. Nasty! Anglos, Francos, Allos . . . what the fuck is that?"

"You happy?"

"Here, I'm happy. Some of these guys I met in a soccer game. They're cool. Nationalists, that's all. Some college kids. Some even studied in the States. They just don't want any fuckin' foreigners telling them what's good for them. And they want to have nothing to do with the Taliban shit, either. They have women fighters amongst them."

"Will they be able to overrun the Taliban?"

"I dunno! You need money to expand. And the warlords are always bringing in more from poppy. You know! So the young folks who wanna fight are going where the numbers are larger and the weapons coming in easier. But let's put it this way—these ISAF troops they call the International Security Assistance Force are going to get hit every day, troop surge or no troop surge. Then the drones retaliate and take out a family. What good is that? You just make more jihadis. When you lose a brother or a sister or a father, you think you're going to sit still and not pick up a Kalash? So we're fighting the Taliban and the ISAF, because the ISAF is busy creating the radicals they want to kill. You get?" He said "we."

I wasn't going to try to persuade him to come back. He had chosen. Like RK had said. It wasn't just good versus bad. Nat understood the complexity, but in his own way.

He had connected the dots and decided he was more useful where he was than back in Montreal.

How would I explain this transformation to Mrs. Meeropol? Where would I begin? I felt that RK had played some kind of role, but I would never really know. I felt both inspired and angry. We chatted for another hour and there was more bread and tea to dip it into.

He wouldn't become the dust that RK had warned about.

"Nat, there is so much you can do by talking about all this in Montreal. I know it sounds irrelevant out here, but this is a time when people back home want to know the facts."

"Me? No! You're the writer. Not me. I'm not a talker, either. What I know is inside. You write about it. If it needs to be written, you do it. Finish your story. You think we're a peace-keeping force? Big fucking myth! A big fucking lie! Canada is here only to show the Americans that we're man enough to dip our hands in Afghan blood. And construction, roads, airports, offices, hospitals, bridges, pipelines, gas storage. That's why we're here."

Eventually the man in black appeared on the doorstep and I heard the van with its engine running. Nat got up first and I followed. He jabbed me lightly on my chest. "You'll be on my mind, man! Yesterday was history, tomorrow is a mystery."

We embraced for a long time. A smile broke through his thick brown beard. The sun moved away from behind a branch in a small tree on top of the hill and appeared like a fugitive, playing games. "See what I mean?" He pointed at the sky. There were no tears. He swung out a short, no-stock Kalash from somewhere behind him and tucked it away under his arms, beneath his shawl. There was a click.

Then suddenly, "You know how RK got his face burnt?" I turned around surprised.

"You know?" I asked.

"Yeah, he told me. He saved a woman in his old country. She had been set on fire by in-laws. He forced her down, rolled her on the floor and put the fire out, but her nylon clothes had attached to his face."

My return plane took off from Kabul on a clear day. The now greenish-blue range was magnificent in the sunlight. One single cloud, small and independent, hovered over a far mountain, its shadow falling on the slope below. There were no other clouds anywhere to be seen. It appeared as if unmoving, stationary. I was convinced it was fated to be there.

CHAPTER TWENTY-FIVE

You Only Live . . . Once

RK's empty urn was in my hands when I arrived at the Montreal International Airport, the ceramic lid taped shut. I placed it on the counter in front of the immigration officer. He asked, in an off-hand manner, what was in the pot. I informed him, with appropriate gravitas, that it was where my grandfather's ashes last resided before I poured them into the River Hooghly in Kolkata. To my surprise he simply waved me on, not even bothering to look for the Afghanistan stamps at the back of my passport.

I, too, had assumed there was nothing inside the pot, but in Amsterdam I had thought to look. Grey ash covered the bottom of the vessel. Apparently not all of RK had been released into the Hooghly. To be frank, I was happy that a part of him preferred to return with me to Canada.

I came out of the sliding doors bearing the urn in my arms, the backpack on a trolley in front. My mother smiled broadly when she saw me. Myra also smiled, more tentatively, then shivered a little and heaved a sigh. When I was closer she put her head on my shoulder, wrapped her arms around me and trembled. Then my mother hugged me. I suppose they really had doubted my return.

Gerry, as usual, had a curt message. "We've got a whole lot to share with you, buddy!"

I wanted to see my grandmother, so we agreed to go there first. Gerry had gotten rid of the Dodge van and replaced it with a Japanese SUV. I shared the back seat with my mother. Myra sat up front with her dad. As we eased out of the airport, I noticed a taxi alongside of us with Nat sitting in the back of it.

I knew I was in Montreal, and he was not. But describing his presence with words like uncanny, magical, or haunting would mean very little; I knew I had left him behind, only to linger on, at his own choice, to make appearances as he wished. From lamppost to street corner, from bars and pubs to culverts along rock-strewn highways, in the mountains and in the shapes of clouds, in the sounds of high heels shuffling along Boulevard St-Laurent and the mortar thump in the green-blue hills, where no one would pass. The Pass. The pass that RK delivered his sermon on. I wasn't so sure who I'd left behind and who had left.

Here there was no blue sky, only grey clouds stretched across the celestial dome. Myra kept looking back at me from the front passenger seat. She finally put out her hand and I held it. I listened carefully but could no longer hear the dull thump of mortars. I looked out as we skimmed along Highway 20. Nothing had changed in the weeks I'd been away: the acoustic baffle walls with their tangle of sculpted inserts and angles, designed to deflect and protect the townhouses from the roar of Highway 20 were intact. Doing their job. Protecting the ears of the gentle residents and still covered with the same colourful, curvaceous graffiti, designed to baffle the mind. Everything was covered up. Everything was packaged and rebranded. Sold as something else. Or simply, the voices that mattered were muffled.

Facts were twisted around and the resulting description was presented as truth.

My grandmother made Darjeeling tea and offered sweets. I was very happy to see her. She looked well. Almost a year had gone by since the death of RK and she seemed to have recovered remarkably. I described in detail how the boat had veered into the river, exactly as RK had described it happening fifty years earlier, and how the ashes poured into its churning womb had swiftly begun their voyage to the Bay of Bengal. She listened and smiled.

That night Myra curled up next to me and we stayed in physical contact all night. I barely slept. At one point I turned my back to her and she made me turn around and lay wrapped in each other's embrace. She looked straight into my eyes. "Whut? Whut are you looking at? What's happening, baby? Are you scared? What is it? *Dis-moi*?"

I didn't tell her that Nat was standing by the foot of the bed, smiling.

CHAPTER TWENTY-SIX

Quels Diables!

Myra looked from the kitchen window to see if anyone was watching at the back parking lot. Then she went to the front balcony windows and did the same. There were no cars anywhere in the next hundred yards or so, engine running or otherwise, with a solitary person in the driver's seat. Then she left through the rear door of the complex wearing a blond wig and a large trench coat. She got into the car in a neighbour's parking lot half a block away and pulled up next to the back entrance in the small rear driveway. I popped into the car as fast as my legs allowed. We pulled away immediately and both of us checked the rear-view mirrors until we reached the main street. She then removed her wig, tossed it into the back and cut loose with a sideways glance at me before punching the air.

How long could we sustain this?

Linda St-Onge's sister allowed us into her life. In the beginning, after Gerry had tracked her down, she'd been leery. She wasn't keen to share the details of her sister's life and death with us, but eventually he convinced her.

We'd arrived the night before, logging several hours past Quebec City before arriving at her modest cottage in Trois-

Pistoles. It was near the Batture sur Plage Morency, muddy brown flats interspersed with mini lakes that slowly emptied into the large river, whose far shore you couldn't see.

She had a single-storey red clapboard house with a white picket fence all around it. Her cottage perched on a hill that sloped to the shore. A boat, with its blue sail rolled tightly against the boom, moored next to a small jetty.

Aurelle St-Onge was drinking coffee and reading a newspaper in the kitchen. She saw me from there and greeted me. *"Bonjour! Avez-vous bien dormi?"*

"Oui, très bien. Merci!" I sat down at the table and she promptly pushed a cup of coffee in front of me with a small jug of milk and a bowl of brown sugar. Myra followed me and very soon all three of us were having pancakes and coffee. Although we all knew there was work ahead, a comfortable weekend feeling enveloped us. For the first time we revealed to someone outside our tight circle what we were trying to do.

Aurelle St-Onge probed with questions and asked what I remembered of having been tossed down three flights of stairs. She asked in a hesitant, sympathetic manner, understanding it might reopen the trauma. I explained to her that I had vague recollections of being clobbered with a padded baseball bat, as well as of a flight path from the third floor, which included my jaws and ribs hitting the railings with sharp clanging sounds before I blacked out completely.

"Quels diables! Je ne peux pas imaginer que les gens puissent en arriver là juste pour obtenir ce qu'ils veulent dans la vie." She was incensed. She shook her head in dismay and then repeated to herself, *"Quels diables!"* The intensity of her feelings was understandable: they had murdered her sister. Although I had not lost anyone close to me, I had been tossed with the clear intent of physical elimination. I have given a lot of thought to this, as you might well understand, and

have discussed the issue with Myra, but the intensity that I witnessed in Aurelle that morning was something I won't forget. It dawned on me that it's one thing to be angry at a single act of crime; it's quite another to be angry that people can get away with that crime and then close the case.

"It's not about a single incident," Gerry had insisted, matter of fact. "It's not about getting even or unravelling a cold case for the adventure of it. The crime of passion is only a small aspect of a major cover-up, one thread within a growing web of deceit."

Aurelle was moved that I had dared to take a job in the Gabriel-Jacops Enterprise, risking my neck to track her sister's killer. I explained it was not our plan to go down without a fight, that we had a journalist on board who had screened the confessional video of Mr. Lips (Mathieu) several times and thought it clear who had contracted the hit men. He was waiting for the final go-ahead to make the big splash. One task remained: securing convincing proof that the plane had been sabotaged.

I sipped my coffee with satisfaction. Unlike in my teen-age years, it now had a welcome flavour in my mouth, even though my jaws were not so well aligned. Aurelle had made a delightful pot.

Nat stood by with a shawl around him and the muzzle of his short stock AK just sticking out a wee bit under the shawl. He was chewing on a flower stalk and smiling.

She had also prepared a map, notes, and pictures to show to us. She started as soon as Myra and I finished the last piece of pancake between us. She said, "I thank you for taking an interest in the unsolved murder of my sister. Rivière-du-Loup airport is located 46 kilometres from Trois-Pistoles, *ici*. That is where Linda's plane was supposed to land, you know." She showed us the exact coordinates as 48° 7' 0" N, 69° 10' 0" W.

And then she showed us another map with a circle around all the areas where parts of the plane had landed, most prominently over the seaway, the reason given for why so much of the plane hadn't been recovered. She then pulled out several documents from a large binder with newspaper clippings in both French and English. Nat leaned over and looked carefully at the map. I looked back at him and Myra caught my eye and put her arm on my shoulder. She knew.

"But after nearly five years since the crash, a local *pêcheur*, Rejean Bolduc, living near l'Isle Verte had found something which he thought was part of the plane. So, he went to discuss with the priest, you know, in our *église*. Now we shall go to see the piece, because I think it's important. There was a— how you say in English?—a cover-up. That *chienne* Corinthe was powerful and she want to take my Linda's husband away and he was crooked too. He was *complice*, you know." She trembled as she said this.

We took our car to the priest's house a few kilometres away. I had the email that Jacques Belanger had sent me long ago.

"An explosive is a substance that does not require oxygen to deflagrate. It ignites on its own." The priest walked around the large oak wood desk to stand closer to us. "One key thing to understand is that explosions liberate a tremendous amount of energy, emit acoustic waves and hot gases, and also shockwaves. So adjacent structures must be able to withstand the shockwave. It is a very rapid oxidation reaction and so it immediately creates a fireball. Therefore, knowledge of explosives and their characteristics is paramount for a forensic scientist involved in such criminal investigations. No explosives expert was called up, no such examinations were carried out, and yet the postman in our village had heard the tremendous sound in the sky. Where had it come from?"

Aurelle must have sensed the questioning in our minds and interjected. "Father Gagnon was an engineer in the Army building bridges, wharfs, and other structures and knows a lot about such things. He was an *ingénieur civil*."

He continued slowly and clearly. "The explosive used in this case is categorized as C-4. It is a high explosive that creates a supersonic pressure wave travelling at more than 340 metres per second. That is the thunder clap the postman heard. C-4 is a plasticized composition of RDX. In my time, these explosives did not exist. In my time we used much simpler explosives, like black gunpowder, ammonium nitrate, or 2,4,6-trinitrotoluene powder. This is a more complex compound—cyclotrimethylenetrinitramine, also known as RDX. Its shockwave could easily put a small plane into a tailspin. It is plasticized, so it can be inserted into fine cracks or small cavities for blasting operations. It is a secondary and quite stable explosive which will not explode on impact. You can stomp on it and nothing will happen. In fact, it requires a primary detonation technique."

"Ah! That's what I wanted to know," I interjected, "because the package the lady gave to me was a simple cardboard box, but very compact, heavy and tight. There didn't seem to be any loose parts in it. Do you think there was a timer in it?" I asked.

"Yes, of course," he continued, undisturbed. "We shall come to that. What is important to know is that in any explosive residue examination, one must build a profile of the explosive used. It is not enough to identify the actual explosive, there's a need to identify the detonation technique, the plasticizer, the binder, as well as other chemical traces like boosters or the taggant, which is an odorizer which enables you to trace the date and point of manufacture. Interesting, is it not? I sent the piece and the report to the National Research

Council in Boucherville where I have an old friend, because the university lab in Chicoutimi was inadequate to build a complete profile. Here is that report."

He pulled out an impressive-looking binder. "And if you look at page seven, you'll see that the taggant traces the source of manufacture and, more importantly, the actual buyer of the C-4!"

The three of us craned over and saw a complicated set of addresses, purchase orders, and delivery notices. Nat leaned against the wall. The final destination was a diamond mining company in the Congo. Aurelle stood and quietly went into the parish kitchen to prepare more tea.

The report asserted that the explosive was the C-4 variety which had a detonation velocity of 8,040 m/s—or as I calculated later, 26,400 ft/s; 28,900 km/h; and 18,000 mph. Obviously, the debris perimeter selected by the investigators was terribly underestimated. Linda St-Onge and five others, including the pilot, had been blown to bits and spread over Trois-Pistoles in a circle that was at least five kilometres in radius, given the height of the plane when it exploded. Nat now stood at another corner of the room, one eyebrow raised. Then he stepped away and I never saw him again.

The Reverend cradled his second cup of tea and restarted the discussion. "Here is a list of the fifty or so pieces that were recovered over a period of time by the salvage crew. You will see that amongst the list is what is described as the back plate of an altimeter dial on the pilot's control panel. Not actually! This is a small section of the folding rest of a Swiss military alarm clock. Pretty much the same as what I have there at the end of the table." Saying that, he went over and picked up the handsome black and grey alarm clock, about two inches in diameter, which had an international calendar clock on its front face. The base was a folding anodized plate and it looked exactly like the picture of the segment shown in the photograph. He had done his homework with astounding precision. It was a simple clock, battery powered with a hand-adjusted timer mechanism. All that was needed was a battery that worked and a couple of lead wires connected to a primary detonator, made of a small amount of not-so-high-tech gunpowder or TNT.

The Reverend smiled thoughtfully. "As they say in English, signed, sealed, and delivered! Only in this case it has been tagged, traced, and waits for deliverance!" He hesitated before going on. " . . . I would have brought this to the attention of the authorities, but it's going to be a difficult, drawn-out process. I am old. I was hoping for someone younger to get involved, and now I have you and the very kind gentleman, Mr. Banks, who seems both well organized and resourceful."

"He's my father!" Myra said with a resplendent smile.

"Can we have a copy of the report?" I asked.

"Certainly! That's the point! I have a second copy. You can have that. I must tell you that I am feeling a bit tired right now. If you will excuse me, I shall retire. I have parishioners to meet later in the afternoon. I thank you for your initiative. Linda used to come here from the time when she was a child. I sincerely miss her."

He gently bowed his head, shook our hands, and walked us towards the large oak door. Aurelle thanked him and we took our leave, with the report under my arm.

"Aha!" said Aurelle as soon as we got into the car. "I wonder who owns the mining company in the Congo, and how their explosives were transferred to the *chienne!*"

CHAPTER TWENTY-SEVEN

The Thaw is Official

The headlines were splashed across *Le Journal de Quebec* ten days later, published simultaneously in Montreal and Quebec City. Cottage-country whodunit, organized crime, and corporate sleaze were all nicely mixed and attractively served up by the journalist Jacques Belanger. It was offered as a three-part series beginning with interviews of Rejean Bolduc, the fisherman who found parts of the downed plane, and Emil Leblanc, the mailman who heard an explosion. It continued with a detailed interview with Father Charles Gagnon, presented as a war veteran and both a man of science and a man of God, a heavy hitter whose critique of the investigation of the downed plane was the "signing, sealing, and delivering" of a bullet-proof conclusion that the plane had exploded which, for some as yet unexplained reason, had been missed by both the provincial police and the federal RCMP. He also offered evidence of widespread procedural problems and specifically asked why the International Civil Aviation Authorities had not been brought in. Photocopied excerpts from the forensic report identifying the chemical explosives were laid out with red balloons encircling references to C-4.

Public interest grew quickly. The paper's print run doubled. Television reporters descended on Trois-Pistoles.

No accusing fingers had yet been pointed, just the evidence that the death of a brilliant Quebec artist in a plane crash had been hushed up, and that the investigating authorities had prematurely declared it a cold case. A factual tone had been set and, in the heat of its glare, the cold case continued to thaw. Journalists, editors, politicians, and TV anchors led themselves in circles wondering where the information would lead. They demanded the chutney and masala, as RK would have said.

The second instalment began where it had left off, with Father Gagnon. He asserted that the taggant of the explosive had been traced and could prove that it had been sold to a diamond mining company in the Congo which was majority owned by Gabriel-Jacops Enterprise Inc., a Quebec company with its head office on Boulevard René-Levesque. This was accompanied with a photo of the majestic, yet gaunt, copper-domed, granite-faced monument to the industrial success of two Quebec families who had merged business interests to create a transnational presence in industrial tooling. But how did the plastic explosives end up in Montreal, the journalist asked, if it was destined for the Congo?

Accompanying this was a shorter human interest interview with Aurelle St-Onge, the dead woman's sister. A moving picture—presented on page two, side-by-side with that of corporate headquarters—of her looking out over the broad, empty river.

"Do you have any idea, why someone would have wanted to hurt her?" the reporter asked.

"I still ask myself that question. Linda would never hurt anyone! Why would anyone want to kill my sister and five other people?"

"Do you know if she had reason to be unhappy? Were there any romantic entanglements? Maybe an affair?"

"I don't know. That's for the police to discover. But why did they close the case so quickly? Why?"

Finally, a passing reference was made to the fact that the artist Linda St-Onge's former husband, Dr. Roberge, a society chiropractor, had married the daughter of the well-known Gabriel-Jacops Enterprise founder. The reporter mentioned he had requested an interview with both Corinthe Jacops and the founder of the Enterprise, but had been refused in both cases.

The third and final episode was the most devastating. It started out with a general description of the Enterprise and its various interests: diamond mines, industrial abrasives, explosives, security agencies, and, more recently, the outsourcing of security services in Afghanistan. The company was presented as a corporate heavyweight with direct access to the Prime Minister's office. The reporter managed to accompany this with up-to-date information on the haunts of the sons and daughter of the founder—the clubs they frequented and the people they knew.

It ended with revelations from Mathieu "Lips" Gelinas, who had recently entered the witness protection program. His links to biker gangs and local street thugs were disclosed, as well as the fact that he had told police the names of the people who had hired his services as an enforcer, including, through well-known intermediaries, one-time employees of the Jacops family. "Lips" also confessed to having roughed up a hapless employee of the company and thrown him down three flights of stairs for being too inquisitive.

The reporter ended the series by pointing to a motive. He noted that Linda had had a life insurance policy worth over a million dollars, and it was Dr. Roberge, now married to Corinthe Jacops, who had collected it.

Tabloids immediately named it Pistoles-gate! Opposition members asked questions, the PM's office issued routine statements refusing to comment on criminal cases *sub-judice*, and new police warrants were issued for searches and questioning. Also, of consequence, the share values of the publicly traded company plummeted and a conversation began as to whether the mining operations in Africa would close.

And that was the turning point. The graded glare of the designer shades, the well-assembled Basra pearl necklace, bobbing arrogantly on a generously contoured Monica Vitti chest, the voluble diesel engine running like a Panzer tank outside, the bleak prospects of denial, distortion, and photo-shopped distraction—all this was not in the realm of possibilities. The Enterprise had been cracked asunder. The HR director was exposed. The paramour was ready to be charged for life insurance fraud. The card house was tumbling.

CHAPTER TWENTY-EIGHT

Blossoms

I looked up and the sky was dark blue. In Kandahar, the poppy fields would be blossoming. Low-energy kids in black, their tawny skins covered by loosely tied greyish turbans, would be plodding through the green fields, their practiced hands reaching for the greenish-pink blossoms bobbing in the radiating heat. Blossoms that no law, no army, no treaties, no shoulder-launched projectiles had as yet been able to control or curtail. Their faces caught in a grimace as they used a special four-bladed knife to scrape the poppy and then later, when the sun had dried out the secretion, return with a curved hook-blade to collect the ooze. The big men would come later to the huts at the edge of those fields to buy the tar from elders in well-practiced quiet transactional tones. Mountain children and their mountain adults. Waiting to be bombed.

I walked on down the pavement of St-Laurent. The sound of kids skateboarding in maroon, blue, and saffron shorts with wrap-around shades and confident smiles pouncing, bouncing, and whirling around guilt-free, like shadowless miracles, creatures of God, unperturbed by the powder that had funnelled through their nostrils. And there were the squealing sounds of young men and women, mostly in their twenties, and occasionally perturbed adults as they pushed and shoved and walked in a phalanx down the pavement, clearing to the side as soon as someone approached; good mannerisms—*Pardon! Pardon!*—as shoulders grazed ever so slightly. Plain children and their plain adults.

The bank on the corner had closed down, leaving behind two unattended ATMs with a glassed-in area which gave welcome respite from the cold for men who drifted hesitantly along the street, coffee cups in hand. Last years' urine odours permeated through the fur-lined doorframes. Flyers swirled about in the small entry leading up to the sports bar above the pastrami deli. I noticed two lots that had been destroyed by fire. One of them was the shish taouk place. The building was still standing, sort of, with a large À *Vendre* sign plastered on it. The other plot across the street had been bulldozed clean. Despite the tidy backstreet parking now visible, it still had a feeling of desolation, a ruin—like a mini bombed-out WWII picture. I couldn't remember what shop had been there. It had already been bombed.

My own turf was slipping away from under me. Whatever had meant something before meant very little now. The mood, the sounds, the ambience, the movie sets, the locales; all had gone pale. The blues strain, the harmonica vamp that floated out of the upstairs bars, the vibrant hellos from barmen and patrons, the historic pictures of the Main laminated into obscure walls were still there, but not there, too.

There was a disparity and unevenness that had built up over years and was now de rigueur, fixed. The evening was clear, unconscious, bewildering, removed, and aseptic. The fog had lifted.

CHAPTER TWENTY-NINE

Blue Skies
and the Colour of Blood!

Myra disabled my distractedness by setting up meetings on regular intervals.

"Okay, today at 3 p.m. we are meeting Leo again. Just to make sure. In the evening, we meet Gerry and his friend who made the film about the Jacops mining empire. Yeeeuh?"

"Friday, you have your physio at 11. We have lunch at the Barn and we leave right away for Lasalle to meet Bélanger. Just so he doesn't introduce fiction to sex up his story. Cool?"

"Saturday, we go to *Downstairs*. Nat's old chum is playing there with a trio." And so on.

Milestones and drop-dead dates, sprinkled in with rest and relaxation. Towards a focused closure, like flies flattened down one by one, briskly, between the pages of a hastily closed diary—to die of suffocation between paper, words, and wisdom. She was as officious as a newly hired office administrator could be. Energizing everyone till I could barely stand it. But going along was the only choice. A plane had been brought down. An artist had fallen from the sky. A con artist had flown away. Someone had pocketed "a shit load of currency." And the usual suspects had also flown away. She was project planning every step of the way, closing loops, closing proofs, building the case. Making it bullet-proof. And in her planner, a quote scribbled on the first page with laborious intensity: "*Through tattered clothes great vices do appear; robes and furred gowns hide all. Plate sin with gold and the strong lance of justice hurtless breaks. Arm it in rags, a pigmy's straw does pierce it.*" I thought it was from King Lear.

Gerry had arranged to screen a Super 8 film in his office. Roland Geddes, the man who had written, shot, and edited it during the 70s, was originally from the Congo but now lived in Montreal. A musician, he had made the film out of conviction. His few introductory words conveyed his bitterness regarding public recognition the film never received. Now in his early sixties, he still spoke French with an African accent as he explained when he had made the film. "*J'avais fait ce film, il y a des années, avant qu'il y ait eu n'importe quel entretien des diamants de conflit.*" He edged out his jaw, as if challenging us to answer the more important questions by watching the work.

Dark hands and feet, injured and with open infections. A boy bending over the river bed. A pan being rocked from side to side. The images rolled along, accompanied by the eerie chattering of sprockets and film. A group of men appears, sitting at a table. Unfortunately the quality of the film deteriorated, sound and colours fading. The men are looking at maps. Close-ups of maps. A voice-over describes the territory where surface diamonds can be found. Suddenly there appears a group of white men, Mr. Jacops and his group. They join the meeting. The voice-over continues: "This man runs Sécure-Afrique, a company that provides perimeter defence for the diamond companies, using mercenaries from different nations. But that is only one of his businesses. He also has a stake in the company that buys the diamonds from these rebel groups. It's that money which finances the wars of these rebels." Then Mr. Jacops and his eldest son are shaking hands with the rebel leader.

When the movie was over, Roland took a sip from the Styrofoam cup he had brought with him, rolled his tongue over his lips and said, "All snakes. All still around. Right here in this city."

I had started to take notes and flattered myself that he appreciated it. Finally, someone was listening. I couldn't help turning back a few pages in my diary to review previous notes from Gerry. "Blue-Sky Inc. was formed in no time." And finally, I understood. Of course, it had been formed quickly, Sécure-Afrique was the precursor to Blue-Sky: from the gritty wet diamond trenches to the dry, IED-infested mountains; from the red soil of Africa to the blue-green mountains and skies over Afghanistan; the organizational structure and intentions were the same. And the result was always the colour of blood.

Mr. Geddes spoke again. "*Les explosifs* used in the mountains surrounding the lakes . . . where the mining is done are imported from another company in Eastern Europe called Salvaggio Exports. They buy *le plastique* from the Czech Republic and then ship it directly to Africa. But I discovered that Salvaggio Exports is a front for a company 100 percent owned by this same Jacops family in Montreal. They used an Italian name to confuse everyone. There is no Salvaggio."

Myra looked at me and I looked at Gerry. He had his legs stretched out and a tight smile on his face. He picked up the thread. "So, I tried to track down the Salvaggio Company and, like he said, it doesn't exist. Except they made a mistake. They do have a P.O. box in Westmount, which just so happens to be the same one used by the daughter of the family."

Myra blurted out involuntarily, "What the fuck! Is she like insane, stupid, or both?"

"*Tous les deux probablement et aussi arrogant!*" affirmed Mr. Geddes, finally relaxing enough to laugh at the thought of her being both. Stupid and arrogant. "So, Mr. Banks and I went to the post office and stuck some wax into the keyhole like we're wartime OSS people, you know! We got the impression in no time. Some back and forth with a locksmith, but no problem. It finally opens up and there is a lot of mail there for Ms. Corinthe and some for Salvaggio Exports."

All eyes turned to Gerry as he pulled out a police badge from his inside pocket and flashed a smile. "We got the details of the owner from the administrator at the counter by showing the badge. Your grandfather and I had the occasion to use it once before when we got hold of Lucky Lips in the alley!"

RK! What a fox!

Myra connected the dots. "So you see, a small shipment of explosives could have been diverted to the Montreal mailbox directly from Prague, instead of being sent to the Congo. That simple."

We left the office and the three of us started back home. Coup de grace, baby.

It was Myra who spotted the car parked on our street with a bulky man sitting inside reading a tabloid. Gerry tensed. He asked Myra not to park but to continue by him. As we came up to pass, the man put his paper down and tried to look at us through his rear-view mirror.

"What now?" Myra was worried.

"We need to take care of him." Gerry decided. "Take the alley, double back; park the car at the corner of the next street over." Myra did exactly that.

"Now we double back, no talking."

We hadn't discussed a plan but Gerry was leading. His walk was measured and quick, more like a trot. He suddenly stopped at the corner and gave us a 1-2-3 operational plan. No questions were asked. For a split second, I had wanted to open my mouth to say something, but nothing came out.

We returned to our street running, crouched. Gerry whipped around the car and opened the door. At the same moment, I lunged in and dragged the man out by the collar of his jacket with a massive pull. He didn't have time to react. He looked at my face as he fell to the side, and I recognized the second man in my apartment. My memory erupted like an engine shifting into full throttle. As he struggled up to lean against the car he was reaching into his jacket but my metal-plated shin bones swung swiftly into his crotch. I kicked again, and this time the toes of my soft-soled shoes connected directly with his lop-sided testicles. He closed his eyes and doubled over just as my knee rose to meet his nose. I said "ouch" somewhere in my mind because I had hurt my knee. His hands went to his face, but Gerry's fist reached it first. The guy fell; straight and heavy like an obelisk, his nose leaking a thick dark scummy liquid.

He was out cold, sputum bubbling from his mouth like a poisonous effluent. I saw him clearly now. It was him. My whole body lurched as it remembered falling backwards down the fire escape as he stood smiling. I kicked him again, and then again. Myra did not stop me, which was a relief.

Gerry picked out the hood's cell from his pocket and called 9-1-1. He told them that two guys were fighting on the street and that one seemed injured. He hung up abruptly, after stating the street name and corner. He wiped the phone carefully with the man's own coat and left it lying with him. Myra whipped out her phone to take pictures of the licence plate, the car, and the contorted face of the man bleeding on the asphalt.

We didn't go into our apartment right away. We returned to our car and then approached our apartment through the underground garage. We heard the wail of sirens outside. I was shaking a bit. I had never fully realized until then the violence I was capable of. Or, was it that I had changed into something else? I had also not known that such an operation could be swiftly carried out by a non-military team with such precision. Gerry went to the sink and insisted we all wash up. Then he sat and poured himself a glass of Bushmill. His eyes closed as he swallowed the drink in one gulp. Then he opened his eyes and shrugged his shoulders.

CHAPTER THIRTY

The Two Things
That Happened in the Beginning

Dishonourable and discredited as they were, they still managed to pull off their escape.

A rather florid description of their unexpected getaway appeared in the tabloid, *Miroir de Montreal:* "The two-storeyed sand-coloured villa has a kidney-shaped swimming pool located just fifteen feet from the large glass doors of the magnificently proportioned family room, which faces south. Beyond it is the azure sea. In the family room are marble statues of Greek goddesses looking out through the chiffon curtains billowing over the remarkable view. That is where the nearly naked bodies of the chiropractor and his society wife, each partially covered by an open white bathrobe, were found hanging from the ceiling fans by their Bahamian butler. He reported it was his job every morning to water the numerous cascades of red bougainvillea flowers that decorated the room."

That night the BBC news announced that a Hellfire missile from a drone had made a successful strike in the hills surrounding Kandahar. It was reported that several extremists had been confirmed killed. It was also mentioned that, according to an as yet unconfirmed rumour, there may have been civilian casualties.

But I was used to that now.

CHAPTER THIRTY-ONE

Not Coming Back

It was his birthday.

I took a cab and arrived at her doorstep at eight in the evening, just as the sun had disappeared abruptly, leaving no indication of reappearing until the next week. She stood at the top of the stairs. The light behind threw a halo around her untidy hair; loose strands of tenderness floated about her face as a reminder of having come here and found one's bearings, built a small livelihood and slowly lost it—and the fan overhead created waves of migrant sadness. The lines and shadows on her face were Afghanistan: incisions and trenches burrowed deep, repeatedly, where once there had been smooth, pastoral placidness. The shine of her forehead had faded. She looked fragile.

I had called her last night to tell her I would come over and she had replied with only one word: "Please." I walked up the last few steps. She offered her arms and then withdrew them suddenly, sobbing. I put my arm on her shoulder and she said, "Sorry." Then she turned and walked away towards the kitchen.

How could Ava Gardner say sorry?

Someone whose legacy is such that she is invariably cast as a resolute survivor; someone who holds together with silence and fortitude in the face of any loss. What a sentence, for a nation, for a people, for a person! For a split second, she had betrayed the turmoil of her emotions, but she was not one to burst into hostile tongues. She never did. Her thoughtfulness and enormous scepticism, combined with a charming demeanour, had always confirmed to me that reason and empathy would triumph in the end.

And yet there she had stood, dismantled, disfigured, sonless, in the darkness of a staircase with the fan turning slowly above. What does it matter who your ancestors were if you do not know where you will go next?

She returned from the kitchen, the teacup tottering as she brought it out with a slice of chocolate cake on a plate. "Today is Nat's birthday," she told me. "Please have some. Darjeeling." She placed the cup and cake on the table.

What does a mother do on her son's birthday when she doesn't know where he is, when there is no one with whom to celebrate? Who else but me would remember the excited discussions, the books read, the stories shared?

It was I who had travelled with her from Brooklyn, from somewhere in Poland—or was it Russia, maybe Germany? It was I who had settled in a cold water flat with her mother while she knitted socks; I who had seen her walking with a spring in her step when Moshe's hat flew off on Bagg Street; I who was there when she got married; and I who had watched as Moshe engraved tombstone after tombstone. And it was I who had seen Moshe lying on the pavement gasping, who had called Nat who had come rushing.

Why the fuck did Nat have to go to Afghanistan and leave us all in despair? There was nothing redeeming about it, not even switching sides to become some *mujahedeen*. What good did it serve? What did it prove? It was their war, their battle! How could he win? For that matter, who would even know where he went? Who would ever find out or care what he had done?

Mrs. Meeropol went back into her bedroom while I slowly, mechanically, and pointlessly dismantled the layered chocolate cake, not knowing what to do next. I had already given her a brief description of my encounter with Nat. I had already informed her that he was convinced he was suffering from trauma and nothing would help him recover. She knew he had gone there as part of a private security outfit and had switched sides to act with the militants in the hills. How could this be anything but a nightmare to her? Through the partly open door I saw Nat's bed still neatly in place, a huge folded duvet covering the bottom of it. Everything tidied, organized, and anticipating.

After a while she came out and sat down, her nose redder than before. She had tidied herself up. She tried hard to smile and asked, "How is Myra?"

"She's good," I replied. "Tell me, has Nat written to you?"

"A long time ago. Perhaps the week you came back. Short note. I don't think he has any plans to return." She looked away as she said that.

"I think he'll come back," I said. "But we'll all have to make our utmost efforts to provide him support. It's going to be a tough ride. He's seen it all."

"I think your grandfather knew that would happen. He was a great man. Nat wrote to me about him, mostly little things. He said Afghanistan turned out to be exactly as he had said it would be; that he had even predicted there would be forces amongst the Taliban with whom we would have to negotiate. And it seems that way now. It is always grey in between."

She was a different woman, no longer the energetic, conspicuously well-informed debater and counsellor. She had become shy, distracted, a citizen of a faraway country, an immigrant yet again. For the first time, I realized that she was nearly seventy years old, perhaps more. I felt bereft and emptied out. My notions about her glamour and command over the challenges of daily life, her resolute upbringing and history, suddenly evaporated.

"Mrs. Meeropol, is there anything I can do to help you? I really don't want to intrude, but you know what Nat has always meant to me."

I saw a crease form between her eyes. Her lips trembled. "Well, you do know that I have always loved you like my own. You do understand that, don't you?"

"Yes, I know."

She shuddered, then put her hand out. "Tell me, can you look after the business? I don't trust anyone else. You can have whatever share you want. I don't care. I just want you around, looking after it."

"Yes, I'll do the best I can. I don't have any interest in shares."

I walked slowly away from her place that night and then hailed a cab to take me home. There was no moon, nor any fog above the Main. The cab made a tight turn onto St-Urbain and headed south.

I reached home and couldn't find Myra. I was surprised because it was late. She had not often gone out since we had moved in together. I immediately switched on the desktop to check for emails. There was only one, from Shaheed, and it had no subject heading.

"Dear Brother Chuck, I regretfully inform you that our brother and fellow freedom fighter, Azmat, was martyred by a missile from a drone fired by the Americans at 11:15 hours

today Afghanistan time. Along with him were martyred two other brothers, several villagers, two women, and a five-year-old child with whom Azmat was playing when the drone struck. Please convey our deepest condolences to his mother, about whom our brother often talked. We send our deepest sympathies to you as well."

I called Mrs. Meeropol and told her I had to come over right away. I hung up after the one sentence to stop her from asking questions. But I think she knew by my voice. My insides were turning over and my forehead felt numbed. My fingers could not hold on to the receiver.

CHAPTER THIRTY-TWO

Double Funeral

RK once took a massive drag on his Bergamot-flavoured cigar and announced that gravitation has no impact on the mind. You can't bend it or force it in one direction. If you spin a coin around, it ultimately settles down to a zero kinetic energy state and the two component forces in the vertical and horizontal—to roll and to spin—are eventually overpowered by environmental friction and gravity. The coin settles to a dead stop.

When you are unconvinced about going to war and yet you wade into it, it's like the fog of war. When you are in a state of indecisiveness and your personality is split, then unexplainable attractions and utter contempt collide. As would a fog of emotions. When you are in exile, a quiet madness seizes upon you. Citizenship means you have to have your feet on two shores. The coin always hobbles to a stop. Not the mind.

As far as I was concerned, there wasn't much of significance being said or done at the service in the Bagg Street synagogue. There was no body to be washed, no casket with holes on the sides to let oxygen or earth enter. Eulogies floated over the audience and evaporated into the benevolent air. The actor had turned soldier, or maybe guerrilla, in a faraway land. He baffled everyone. Had he been a turncoat? Had there been a conversion? Was it convincing? Had the seeds of it been there all along? Who had seen the signs? Those were the questions in the lanes and streets outside, but not as part of a genuine conversation on how it might have happened. Rather, as a playful dance of words to avoid the issues.

Not even the death by drone of one of our own could bring the situation home.

The reality of Afghanistan was not in the heads of the colourful groups who trooped down St-Laurent past the synagogue, careless flesh overflowing their purple and green dresses, licking quickly at the sides of their ice cream cones, stopping and staring at those of us gathered for the service, wondering who had met his maker.

A soldier died. No, no, not a soldier, an actor from the neighbourhood. Wrong! A fighter from Afghanistan. Afghanistan? What was he doing there? Whose side was he on? The service is in a synagogue? Yup! 'Cos he was a Jew. No body, though, because he was blown up by an IED. Ha! It was not an IED, it was a missile from a drone. No! Really?

And on. Did he convert? Did he get radicalized?

Inside, the hubris of eulogies encrusted with a thick varnish of local hypocrisy overflowed; sentimental hyperbole poured out about the most trivial aspects of his life. His final call, his last actions, was scrupulously avoided. He had perished where no one on the Main would ever have gone. It added to his allure as an eccentric, an original, a local hero. And so, he was to be released from the Main like a Hollywood idol who had died prematurely.

I overheard the usual suspects whispering about "what really went wrong" and "what a shame" in spite of his "wonderful family." To them, his conversion was inconceivable.

I knew that his vitality and resolution went everywhere with him. I knew that he learned by himself and worked from there. Too much was *trop* for him. In Kandahar, he had done what he did on the Main: quietly learning what was what, going about it with courage, and asserting his beliefs quietly but firmly. Nobody talked about that. Maybe because nobody knew.

I was lucky to have made the journey to see him, to remember him smiling in the middle of a parched terracotta field. I considered myself a changed man, having avenged the murder of Ms. St-Onge. Having thawed out the cold case, with the help of others. There was humanity left. Some justice was still available.

The local city councillor insisted on saying a few words on how Nat was known in the neighbourhood as a do-gooder. "He raised funds for community activities! Organized street fairs!" Of course, this feckless jackass didn't have the gumption to state that Nathaniel Meeropol came from an idealist legacy: his great-grandparents in Russia were people who were selfless, involved, excited by thoughts of righteous change; folks conspiratorial by tradition who planned revolts, organized change on the side of the rabble, and remained unabashed in their dissent with the status quo. I listened to his lack of historical consideration, his inability to expand his one-dimensional imagination. His horrendous misrepresentation continued. Why was I getting angry? Why had rage begun to race through my veins?

Mrs. Meeropol insisted I speak. "Tell it like you feel it, Chuck. Please." She said it clearly, with trepidation perhaps, but not doubt.

I spoke. The first ten minutes were about how we had grown up together. The Rebbe had tears in his eyes when I described how Nat had stood alone at the corner of Bagg

Street after Moshe Meeropol had passed on; his shirt untucked, a cigarette hanging lose from his lips, looking down at the street. And I recounted how when I'd put my arms around him he had said, "Whoa! Let's go get a beer!" And everyone there smiled, because what I said fit, they knew him just like that. I was telling it like it was.

Then I told them about Afghanistan and exactly what he had said, in the few words he had used. There was a stunned silence. I insisted they were not my words—they were his words. And a few people nodded, knowing that would be true. I repeated exactly what he had told me, "We got no business here! Canada's got it all wrong."

I told them that Nat was a man who had, at the end of his life, lived beyond the Main, had travelled to where his ancestors had lived. I told them, "He went to Kandahar, where the Karakoram, Kunlun, and Hind Kush met the Pamir and the Himalayas, and the collision created the roof of the world. He had gone where the Tajiks met the Persians, the Pashtun, the Kadjar, the Kyrgyz, and the Uighur—where travellers, his ancestors, had navigated between the Caspian and the Black Sea and moved back and forth seeking new societies and freedoms."

"No country," he had said, "should ever be party to such missions of falsehoods as 'Enduring Freedom.'" I looked at my grandmother when I said this. She was there with my parents. She knew where it came from. RK and Nat had merged and were going to leave together. It was a double funeral. The end of two stories. The plane crash and the drone strike.

I didn't know where my voice was coming from, but I couldn't hold it back. I held the podium and looked at the people in front. Everything was out of focus, as if a sheet of water separated me from them. There were over two hundred people from all corners of the Main. At the back stood the bartenders, the fly artists who had removed their hoodies this one time, walkers, film editors, agents, club owners, store keepers, those with no known address, the activists from the local anti-poverty coalition, his past girlfriends and, yes, Myra, all sitting there and looking straight at me. Even a few bouncers turned up and together held their hands to their chests in salute.

Later I sat like a child next to Mrs. Meeropol, my head staring up at the ceiling.

When we stepped out, it was as if the entire neighbour-hood had turned up outside. The police had sent a few squad cars, just in case. Family members from Brooklyn had arrived late and were moping around, lost. Mrs. Meeropol did her best to greet the family.

Gerry left for Africa the week after sitting shiva, intent on resuming his work with the laptop distribution project in African schools. Myra and I took him to the airport, hugged each other, and fell silent. Finally, he said, "I'm happy you've found each other." We wished him well.

We drove back from the airport without a word being spoken between us. She went into the bedroom and lay down. I put my legs up on the coffee table in the living room and fell asleep.

I started to work four days a week at the Meeropol Monument Company. I took the orders, talked to the clients, engaged the workers, kept the books, ordered the marble, called up the truckers, walked around the tombstones, and inspected the writing. I felt the tombstones to ensure there were no sharp edges and ensured that all the writing, the star, the lion, or the scroll, was uniform and well centred.

Mrs. Meeropol came twice a week, and I often went back to her house and had dinner with her. She had lost weight and looked drawn. We didn't discuss Nat anymore. She often sat on a long easy chair with her eyes closed, looking out at the sun as it streamed through a stained-glass section in her library. The colours fell on her face and, to me at least, Ava Gardner again lay there, Chagall-ed and segmented. I updated the computer in her house with key figures every week and she perused them. There were seven employees on the payroll, and I finally arranged for automatic deposits. She paid me more than the Enterprise or my old courier company had done. In the beginning the workers were not fond of me, but they soon realized that Mrs. Meeropol treated me like family. If they had problems she'd say, "Ask Chuck."

I walked to St-Urbain and took the bus to the metro on my way home. I no longer felt unsafe in any way. Perhaps I didn't really care.

Reporters approached to do a profile of me in relation to the scandal involving two Montrealers who committed suicide in the Bahamas. They wanted to start by saying that I was the son of the owners of a well-known fusion restaurant on Guy. I told them to take a long hike in a large forest in a very distant land. When I told her that, Ruth Meeropol had smiled and even giggled.

One evening I came home and Myra was walking around in high heels, a scarf around her neck, pacing the apartment. Her eyebrows were raised and she had changed her hairstyle. I tried to talk to her, but she wouldn't answer.

A week later I returned home early and noticed she wasn't there. I hoped she had picked up a voice-over advertising gig somewhere. She was beginning to get those types of contracts lately. They liked how she could capture different personalities, all with a distinct and individual voice. I slumped down on the couch and fell asleep.

The door opened around midnight. I saw Malia framed against the door, the black dress on, the hair raised on both sides of her temples. She looked down at me on the couch. The blue light in the lobby shone through her dress. She did not know me. Agony swept through me.

I stepped out into the blustery night and hailed a cab. I hadn't shaved for a few days and my stubble felt like a mat. When I arrived on St-Laurent, it was choking with people. An outdoor stage had been set up in one of the back lanes. I watched as a band slowly prepared for its second set. I went to the café at the corner of Napoleon, but the line-up was too long. Instead, I sat on the steps outside, took my hat off, and crossed my hands around my knees. I looked at the row of street lamps glowing dimly, and then gazed up at the moon with its halo around it.

Then a woman walked by in torn fishnet stockings and red lipstick. She looked at me and dropped a loony into my hat. The coin spun for a while, then hobbled to a halt.

END

Acknowledgements

There is no moment of doubt. There is a continuum of internal conflicts. What we say we are and what we do not feel comfortable bringing up. What is easily said and done and what is difficult to live by. We are caught in a web—our public stands and our private angst. About not letting the world know, our deepest fears. About hiding behind a smokescreen, a pall of non-descript inanities, a fog cover—behind which we make ourselves acceptable to the public. We play safe. We live between two aspirations. One that we really wish we could live by and what we actually live. This novel is about that conflict. About crossing over to the other side. It is not easy.

I have had some very good well-wishers, close friends and writers who have read the manuscript for this novel, in its various versions. It has gone through many changes. I would like to thank them first. Lisa Foster, Mark Silverman, Michael Springate, Julian Samuel, Cora Siré, Sylvie Martel, Rimi Chatterjee, Jody Freeman, Deirdre Silverman, Sam Boskey, Maya Khankhoje and a few others who read excerpts from it. Every single comment they made or the hesitation they expressed, registered in my brains. I wish to thank Robin Philpot, my publisher at Baraka, for taking up this challenge and also deeply acknowledge the sound advice and guidance I have received from my colleagues at Montreal Serai, who for thirty-two years have been at the core of my literary endeavors.

Printed by Imprimerie Gauvin
Gatineau, Québec